To
Rossi

may you always
be as charming
as your Nono
John

The
Junk-Drawer
Corner-Store
Front-Porch
Blues

JOHN R. POWERS

The Junk-Drawer Corner-Store Front-Porch Blues

A DUTTON BOOK

DUTTON
Published by the Penguin Group
Penguin Books USA Inc., 375 Hudson Street,
New York, New York 10014, U.S.A.
Penguin Books Ltd, 27 Wrights Lane,
London W8 5TZ, England
Penguin Books Australia Ltd, Ringwood,
Victoria, Australia
Penguin Books Canada Ltd, 10 Alcorn Avenue,
Toronto, Ontario, Canada M4V 3B2
Penguin Books (N.Z.) Ltd, 182–190 Wairau Road,
Auckland 10, New Zealand

Penguin Books Ltd, Registered Offices:
Harmondsworth, Middlesex, England

First published by Dutton, an imprint of New American Library,
a division of Penguin Books USA Inc.
Distributed in Canada by McClelland & Stewart Inc.

First Printing, February, 1992
10 9 8 7 6 5 4 3 2 1

Copyright © John R. Powers, 1992
All rights reserved

 REGISTERED TRADEMARK—MARCA REGISTRADA

LIBRARY OF CONGRESS CATALOGING IN PUBLICATION DATA:

Powers, John R.
    The junk-drawer corner-store front-porch blues / John R. Powers.
        p.   cm.
    ISBN 0-525-93405-7
    I. Title.
PS3566.087J86   1992
813'.54—dc20   91-26025
                                                                      CIP

Printed in the United States of America
Set in ITC Century Book
Designed by Leonard Telesca

PUBLISHER'S NOTE
This is a work of fiction. Names, characters, places, and incidents either are
the products of the author's imagination or are used fictitiously, and any
resemblance to actual persons, living or dead, events, or locales is entirely
coincidental.

Without limiting the rights under copyright reserved above, no part of this
publication may be reproduced, stored in or introduced into a retrieval system,
or transmitted, in any form, or by any means (electronic, mechanical,
photocopying, recording, or otherwise), without the prior written permission of
both the copyright owner and the above publisher of this book.

In loving memory of my mother,

June R. Powers

who spent her life strongly encouraging me
to be a human being and, failing that,
a writer.

And to my father,

John F. Powers

Thanks for the footsteps.

Acknowledgments

Thanks to the members of my family for their love and friendship:

My brother, Randy. My sisters, Gaye and Margo Sorrick, my brother-in-law, Ken Sorrick, my nephew and nieces, Joseph, Randy Marie, and Danielle.

A few moments of this book were presented in a teleplay, "Going Home," produced by WLS ABC Televi sion, in Chicago. I would especially like to thank the producers, Pam Whitfield and Tina Hergott, as well as Mike Wall, the director, and the other members of the production staff—Joe Blanford, John Clarke, Bob Pasquale, Annivar Salgado and Ford Swanson. Terry Shapiro did a wonderful job on the still photos. Also, thanks to Joel Ahern, Tim Bennett and Charlotte Koppe for helping this show to happen.

Portions of this book were presented in a one-person show, "Scissors, Paper, Rock." The first reading of the show was graciously hosted by the people of the Downers Grove Library, Downers Grove, Illinois. "Scissors, Paper, Rock" was originally performed at Bradley University in Peoria, Illinois, thanks to Dr. James Ludwig, Chairman of the Drama Department. Thank you, Steve Sturm, for your wonderful direction. The show was next performed at St. Ambrose College and was delightfully produced by Menno Kraii, Director of the Galvin Fine Arts Center. "Scissors, Paper, Rock" was again performed at Chicago's Northeastern Illinois University through the efforts of both the faculty and students of the Speech & Performing Arts Department.

Thank you, Margaret Basch, for all your help.

The artistic coordinator and major moving force behind "Scissors, Paper, Rock" was my dear friend, Libby Adler Mages, whose attitude and life can be summed up in her favorite word, "Hurrah!"

A world of thanks to the three ladies I live with—the three ladies who are my world: my wife, JaNelle, and my daughters, Jacey Elizabeth and Joy Victoria.

The Junk-Drawer Corner-Store Front-Porch Blues

1

I am sitting across from the largest woman I have ever seen: six-and-a-half feet tall and easily as wide. Though she has the stature of an elephant, she speaks with the tiny voice of a mouse. Her name is Minnie. Honest to God.

Minnie is taking my medical history. She's wearing a white uniform. An old joke. "She's so big that, when she wears white, people park in front of her and look for the speakers." I open my spiral notebook and jot it down. Maybe I can rework it so that no one recognizes it for the tired line that it is.

"Mr. Cooper, did you hear my question?" Minnie asks politely. Another annoying thing about Minnie. She's as sweet as apple pie. A very, very large apple pie.

"I'm sorry."

"How many cigarettes do you smoke a day?"

"How do you know I smoke?"

"Well, Mr. Cooper," Minnie the eight-hundred-pound mouse explains, "the kind of cancer you're being tested for is almost always caused by smoking."

"Oh. A little over a pack a day."

As Minnie leans over the desk, her shadow engulfs me. "How little over a pack?"

"Oh, I'd say, about another pack."

Minnie holds the form up in front of her face. "You list your height as six feet." Her eyes peek suspiciously over the paper.

"I'm a very short six feet . . ."

". . . And you're a very heavy one hundred sixty pounds," says Minnie. "No matter. We can verify both before we give you the tests." Minnie begins running her finger down the sheet of paper. "Anyone in your family have cancer?"

"No."

"Heart disease?"

"My father . . . my mother," I reply.

"Allergies to any medications?"

"I don't respond well to antihistamines," I say. "They make me very sleepy."

"That's a normal reaction."

". . . They also make me very depressed. The last two times I bought nasal spray, I tried to kill the pharmacist."

Minnie looks at me, shocked. Then, as she remembers, she smiles at me weakly as she goes back to her questions. "That's right, Mr. Cooper, you're a comedy writer, aren't you?"

"Yes, I am."

"Uh-huh."

I reach for my spiral notebook but Minnie tosses me a glance, which clearly states I have said nothing worthy of writing down. So I don't.

"Any problems with your prostate?" Minnie asks.

"Well, in my work you do a lot of that . . . No, no problems."

"How many times do you urinate a day?"

"I don't know. . . . At my age, half the time I'm asleep . . ." I keep forgetting. Minnie may be a large audience but she isn't necessarily an appreciative one. "I don't know."

"Do you have bowel movements on a daily basis?"

"Ah . . . I can't set my watch by them, if that's what you mean."

Minnie sits back in her chair. "Mr. Cooper, I realize that in your line of work, heckling is an occupational hazard. But we in the medical profession aren't accustomed to it."

"Sorry."

Minnie returns her attention to the forms but then thinks better of it and puts them down on the desk. "I can get the rest of this information later. Let's review the procedure again. After the additional tests and X rays, the doctor will perform the biopsy at the clinic this afternoon. We should have the results by tomorrow afternoon."

"It's going to be a long twenty-four hours. . . ." I glance at the clock. It's not even nine-thirty yet. "More like thirty hours."

Minnie shrugs helplessly. "That's the best we can do, Mr. Cooper." She checks over the form one more time. "Oh, I see that today's your birthday. Happy birthday." She begins to hand me a slip of paper. "Take this to Room Twelve-B for your barium enema."

Before I can react, Minnie yanks her hand back and laughs. "A birthday joke. Hey, I can be funny, too, you know."

* * *

Lying on an operating table, looking up at a herd of medical marauders. Thinking of that wildlife special on PBS last night. All these lions are flopped around this freshly killed zebra gorging themselves into oblivion.

One of the nurses is rubbing a salve into her hands as she explains to another one, "This stuff really helps the stiffness." I recognize the fragrance.

I'm fourteen and Danny's eleven. Getting ready for bed. Danny and I had just had an argument a few minutes earlier. I can't even remember what it was about. He has already gotten into bed and I'm sitting on the edge of mine, rubbing a heat-inducing salve into my knee. I had strained it that afternoon when I had slipped on the grass at the park.

Danny leans his head on his hand as he watches me. "I'd be careful with that stuff if I were you."

"Thanks for the warning," I say sarcastically. "I'll make sure I don't eat too much of it." I can feel my knee begin to glow with heat as the salve penetrates it.

Danny rolls over on his side, away from me, and pulls the covers up to his chin. I think I hear him giggling.

A few moments later, I put the tube on the nightstand and slide under the covers. The knee is really beginning to heat up.

About two minutes later, I notice my ear tingling, then my cheek, the back of my neck, my elbow and parts I don't even want to think about. Apparently, the residue of the salve had remained on my fingers and had left its imprint on every part of my body that I had touched since then.

There are fires breaking out all over me. Leaping

out of bed and running to the bathroom. As I pass Danny's bed, I hear him say, "A little touchy tonight, aren't we?"

The doctor is explaining the procedure as he does it. "Basically, we have inserted a long tube down your throat and into your lung. At the end of this tube is a small snipping device, which will allow me to cut and retrieve a tiny sample of your lung tissue. . . ."

The voice doesn't sound familiar but, after all, it's been thirty-five years.

In fifth grade, during lunch, I deliberately take a bite of a raw onion and then breathe into the face of Theodore Cross, the brightest kid in class and the meekest. Until that moment.

Apparently, my breath inflames more than Theodore's nostril hairs. He grabs me by the front of my shirt and slams me up against the wall. "If you ever do such a despicable thing again," Theodore hisses into my face, "I will reach down your throat and pull out your lungs."

Theodore Cross had always talked about becoming a doctor. Squinting through the tears of pain up at the face of the masked man hovering over me. Could be.

The nurse tells me that it will help ease the pain if I fill my mind with pleasant thoughts. I think of having a cigarette.

2

Today has been one of those Southern California days where the moment you step out of the air-conditioning the heat of the sun rains down on you. Within seconds, you are bleary-eyed from exhaustion as you almost stagger to the next oasis of cool air.

Even now, in the darkness of the evening hours, the air is still wrinkled with heat. I am dreading going into my apartment. The previous night had been cool and, this morning, before I had left for the doctor's, I had forgotten to turn on the air-conditioning. My throat is sore from the tube that had been stuck down it, and I'm getting a headache from the anesthetic.

But as I open the door, a cool wave of air caresses me. In the darkness, one candle burns atop a small cake in the center of the table. Behind the glow of the candle sits the silhouette of Rita. "Happy Birthday, Kidder."

Walking over to Rita. Standing behind her and putting my arms around her neck. "Thank you, all-knowing one, for this light in the darkness." My spiral notebook bumps her in the head.

"Will you put the damn notebook down?"

"Sorry." Tossing it on the table, I sit down on the chair next to her.

"I would have invited all your friends," she says, "but the room's too small."

Another jab at the fact I live in a studio apartment.

I say, "You couldn't fit three people in here?"

"You have very fat friends."

I automatically take out a cigarette, but then the soreness of my throat reminds me of the day's events and I'm about to put it back in the pack. But the gesture alone is enough to light Rita's annoyance.

"Couldn't you let me breathe for just a few minutes before you start puffing on one of those things?"

Sliding the cigarette back into the pack. "Rita, you're absolutely right."

She smiles. "I'm glad to see that you're finally starting to listen to me."

"This isn't really my forty-fifth birthday," I say. "When I was ten years old, I fell asleep and the last thirty-five years have been a dream."

"Maybe they have all been a dream. But what if you were seventy-five when you fell asleep?"

"Thanks for the cheery thought." I get up and pull open the drapes, which reveal a twinkling view of the valley below.

Staring at the view. Wondering why she doesn't ask me how the tests have gone but then remembering that I hadn't told her about them. "So where are the balloons?"

"I didn't buy any," Rita says. "You'd just suck

the air out of them and then talk in that ridiculous voice."

I turn to respond. "No, I wouldn't."

"That's what you did last year."

"I've matured." I know it's a mistake the moment I say the word. I go back to looking out the window.

"Oh," says Rita, standing, "are we going to talk about your maturity level now?"

"It's my birthday. I don't have to talk about anything I don't want to talk about on my birthday."

Rita ignores the remark. "I know I told you we wouldn't talk about this again and, after tonight, I'm afraid we won't. We've been seeing each other for three years now. I'm thirty-seven years old. I have a birthday coming up, too. If I'm going to have a family, it has to be soon. . . . I would appreciate you looking at me when I talk to you."

Continuing to stare out at the view. "It's dark in here. I wouldn't be able to see you anyway."

Rita flips on the light switch. I turn around. "Donald," she says emphatically. From "Kidder" to "Donald" in less than two minutes. Not a good sign. "I'm not asking you to marry me or even suggesting that we live together. But I have some choices to make. What I do want to know is where you see this relationship going?"

"It's not 'going' anywhere. It is," I say.

"Not going anywhere?" The jump in volume of Rita's voice has just raised the ante.

God, am I stepping in it tonight. "That's not what I meant and you know it. What I meant was that our relationship is fine just the way it is now, isn't it?"

"No. A relationship is either growing or dying. Nothing stays the same."

"You know I love you," I say. I automatically take out a cigarette and go to light it. But Rita's glare and my sore throat convince me to snap it in half and toss it into an ashtray. Besides, maybe it is too late, but I want to quit anyway.

"Words are cheap," says Rita.

"You sound like the guys I write for."

Rita again ignores the remark. "You're forty-five years old. It's time you grew up."

"Are you saying I can't make a commitment?"

Rita laughs.

Good God, I've done it again.

"Commitment," she says. "Commitment? Half the time, when you spend the night at my place, you don't spend the night at my place. You leave before morning."

"I really don't like that cat of yours," I explain. "Just when I'm about to fall asleep, it always makes it a point to walk on the piano keys. Rita, have you ever noticed that all cats play piano, but not very well?" Looking for my spiral notebook. "Maybe I can use that."

"The feeling is obviously mutual. My cat never goes near you."

As I write I say to Rita, "Usually, I like cats. But yours is so sneaky. I just don't trust it."

"Then don't borrow money from it." Rita is really working up a head of steam. "Look at the way you live." Rita walks around the corner to the kitchen. I can hear her opening the refrigerator.

"Come here, look at this."

Staying put. "What's your point?"

"My point? There's nothing in the freezer. Nothing. Not even an ice-cube tray. In the refrigerator, there's one apple and a half a bottle of Coke. And you hate apples." Listening to her close the refrigerator while simultaneously opening the cabinet doors.

"Your cabinets have one package of paper plates,

unopened, and two glasses. I brought over the two glasses. That's it."

She charges back into the living room. "A motel room has more warmth than this place. You don't have enough clothes to fill a decent suitcase. Of course, how would you know? You don't own a decent suitcase."

"Now that's not true. . . ."

"Glad bags are not considered quality luggage." Rita starts pacing.

"Hey," I say, "I only used those bags one time and that was because the handle on my suitcase broke. I was driving. It wasn't like I used plastic bags at an airport. Glad bags . . . quality luggage. That's a good line. Where's my notebook?"

"Oh, that's right," says Rita, "make money on my anger."

I grab the notebook and scribble just the words *Garbage bags, luggage.* I say, "You know if I don't write it down right away I'll forget it."

Rita begins calming down, which is not necessarily a good sign. "That's what you and I should do, Donald, forget it."

"You make it sound as if I'm some kind of bum . . . some drifter . . ."

"Emotionally, you are. Even the work you do doesn't demand much commitment. You write one-liners for comedians. Do you know how many times, since I've known you, you've told me you were going to start a novel?"

"How many times have I told you," I counter, "that I have to first come up with a topic that I feel strongly enough about to devote that kind of time and effort to?"

Rita walks over to the table and picks up her purse. She laughs. "I don't even know why I'm wasting my breath." Gesturing. "The furniture's rented. You can't even make a commitment to a couch."

Rita begins walking toward the door.

"Ah, come on, hang around. It's my birthday."

"I'm not 'hanging around.' I'm leaving, Donald."

Stall. If I can get her talking about something else, maybe I can still save the night. "Are you still going with me to see Brian in that stock production next week?"

Rita stops, with her hand on the doorknob. "You know, if he wasn't your son, I think you'd let him float away, too."

"That's a cheap shot." God, would I like a cigarette.

"You're right, it is," she says. "You're a good father . . . and a good comedy writer." Rita turns and opens the door. "But I already have a father and I don't need any more laugh lines."

"I tell you what," I say. "Tomorrow night, let's you and I drive up to the mountains."

"For the tenth time," says Rita slowly, "this is the weekend I'm attending my family's annual reunion in Akron, Ohio. You know, the reunion you always have an excuse for not attending?"

"Rita, you know how busy I've been lately . . ."

She begins opening the door. "Give me your excuses when I get back. In fact, you don't even have to bother then."

"Hey, where's my birthday gift?"

"It's walking out the door."

And so it did.

Rita doesn't even say good-bye. She must really be mad. She knows I hate that more than anything. How can people do that? How do they know they'll ever see each other again? Cold. Very cold.

Turning back to look at the view. I debate about

going after her. But we've had this discussion many times before. I know I am running out of chances but . . . Knowing who you are is one thing. Changing it is quite another.

Can't see the view with all the glare. Going over to the door and turning off the lights. Neither of us had noticed. The candle's gone out.

After eating the chocolate cake, I go out and buy a gallon of chocolate chocolate-chip ice cream. Sitting on the balcony, looking out at the lights, the TV playing behind me. Some people are boozers. Some do drugs. When I get depressed, I try to sweeten myself to death.

Forty-five years old. One ex-wife, one son, one room, one gallon of ice cream. When you're a kid, you tell everybody it's your birthday. As an adult, you tell fewer and fewer people. After enough birthdays, you try forgetting to tell yourself.

The phone calls dwindle. Now, for me, it's only two. Brian and Ma. Brian forgot this one. It happens. Sometimes his mother reminds him. Sometimes she doesn't. But Ma hasn't called either. That never happens.

Thinking about how Dad must have celebrated his forty-fifth. I can't remember that one particular birthday but all family birthdays were a cause for major celebration. The honoree got the dinner of his or her choice. Big cake. Small gifts. Lots of people. Lots of laughs.

Maybe Brian doesn't want to talk to me.

Two months ago, I drive to a small summer stock theater where Brian is working. Picking him up in front of the white farmhouse where the cast is staying. A gravel road runs out of the back of the property, through a wooded area, and up to the side of the little theater, which is about half a mile away.

The moment he gets in the car I start pitching. "Brian, all through high school and college, you've been a straight *A* student. You can be anything you want to be—"

"And I want to be an actor."

"But acting professionally is a lot different from acting in school productions."

"Dad, you asked me to double major and I did."

"I was right, wasn't I? Don't you feel better knowing you have that degree in accounting?"

"Let's put it this way, Dad. I'm not worried. If things don't work out in accounting, I always have my drama major to fall back on."

Pulling up in front of the theater, which doesn't look that much different from the farmhouse, we get out of the car and Brian informs me that the only way to get to the backstage area is to walk through the theater.

Stepping through the doors, we are engulfed by a gray darkness. Light seeps around the edges of the black paper that has been taped to the windows. About two hundred folding chairs make up the audience area. A large stage fills the back of the space.

During a phone call earlier that week, Brian had told me that the theater had been built in the late eighteen hundreds, but that, in recent years, it had been used as a storage area by local farmers. Only in the past few summers had it been converted back to a theater for the summer stock season.

As the doors close behind us, Brian simply stands in the back of the theater, apparently savoring the atmosphere. "I always come this early," he says, "so I can take a few moments to remind myself why I'm here."

"Okay, why are you here?"

Brian speaks softly and with reverence, as if he is in a church. "In about an hour, people will come in and sit down, not really knowing what to expect. I, and my fellow actors, will go out on that stage and create a magic carpet. We will seize their spirits and take them for a ride through their imaginations. A ride that some of them, perhaps, have not taken since their early childhood.

"When we bring them back, when they leave this theater, they will be a little more alive than when they came in. Of all the tens of thousands of days they live in their lives, this is one of the few they will always remember."

What a dreamer. Do I have my work cut out for me. We begin walking through the theater and into the backstage area.

It is a typical summer stock theater. There are only two large dressing rooms, one for the men and one for the women.

As we step into the mens' dressing room, Brian begins organizing his costume, props, and makeup bottles.

"Dad, I really can't talk right now. I've got a lot to do. The other guys will be getting here soon, too."

Brian sits at the long table and begins tinkering with his makeup. I talk to the reflection in the mirror.

"Brian, acting is fun, I know that . . ." I don't. "But it's not the kind of thing you do for a living. For most people in high school and college, acting is just an extracurricular activity, that's all."

"Dad, what other people choose to do with their—"

"You don't try and make a living with an extra-curricular activity."

"Dad, you're not making any—"

"It's . . . it's like making a career out of glee club."

"Dad, it's what I love to—"

"You want to spend your whole life pretending. That's a real world out there. You're not a kid anymore. Becoming an . . ."

Brian forces himself to speak slowly and emphatically as if he is the father and I the son. "Dad, haven't you always told me that I should grow older but never grow up?"

"Well . . . yeah . . . but this isn't what I meant. What I meant . . ."

Brian begins shaking the small bottles of makeup with one hand while dabbing a small brush into a paper cup of water. "I thought you came here to see the show, and me, not lecture me." He turns and looks at me. "This is what I want to do."

"You're going to be a professional liar. That's what actors are, professional liars. If that's what you want to do, why not go into a field where you can make a lot of money doing it: law, advertising, politics . . ."

"Dad, you're not exactly a member of the establishment. You write comedy for a living."

"What's that got to do with lying?"

"Well, that's sort of lying."

This kid is more demented than I thought. "No, Brian. Writing comedy is not 'sort of lying.' Comedy is truth. It's the only truth we have. I mean, in this world, we're all liars to a certain degree. But if everyone told the truth, there wouldn't be any comedy."

"Dad, I'm not demeaning what you do for a living. But I just don't think that comedy is the same as serious acting."

I don't say it but I think it. Serious, my ass. Serious actor. It's a contradiction in terms. The Academy Awards. Never watch them. They almost always give the awards to "serious" works because they know we all want to believe that life is meaningful. But we all laugh at comedy because we strongly suspect that it's not.

"You know, Brian, there are people who think that actors are . . . empty glasses. They're nothing until a writer fills them with a role."

Brian plays his ace. "Mom thinks it's a good idea."

"Mom? That woman just got married for the fourth time. All that rice bouncing off her head is beginning to affect her brain."

"Grandma thinks it's a good idea, too."

"You're going to listen to a seventy-three-year-old woman?"

"I should listen to a forty-seven-year-old man?"

"I'm not even forty-five yet."

Other kids begin drifting into the dressing room. The stage manager, another kid, walks by and yells, "Half hour." I tell Brian that I'll see him after the show, but I don't think he hears me. He's talking to somebody else.

Sitting in the theater watching the show. Looking at the faces of the audience and the cast. Tonight the only one who takes a ride on the magic carpet is Brian.

No more ice cream and my throat's really beginning to kill me. Still worried about Ma, I call her but there's no answer. Maybe she fell asleep early. If she left the television on she wouldn't hear the phone.

Ma's at that age where things are beginning to happen. A couple of years ago, she had a mild heart attack. I got that call at three in the morning.

Lying down in front of the television. Chocolate chocolate-chip racing through my body. I can almost hear the arteries blocking up. Who cares. Dozing off. In the morning, maybe I'll be ten again.

Ringing. I wake up instantly and look at the clock. Only 10:00 P.M. But midnight in Chicago. Could be trouble. I'm like Ma. When I was a kid and the phone rang in the middle of the night, Ma would always be afraid that somebody had died. Dad would want to make sure that somebody did. "Hello?"

"Is this Mr. Donald Cooper?"

"Yes . . ."

"Is your mother named—"

"Please get to the point."

"Sorry. Your mother's named Mary?"

"Yes."

"Well, I'm Dr. Logan, calling from Simone Hospital in Chicago. Your mother's taken a rather bad fall. . . ."

"How bad?"

"Well, no head injuries. But she did break her hip. Or it might have just given way. I'm not really sure. A badly bruised arm but no breaks there. Now she asked us to call you but wanted us to make sure you understand that there's no need for you to come to Chicago. She told us she has relatives here . . . cousins, in-laws, that sort of thing. . . ."

"Is she awake now?"

"Pretty heavily sedated but she should be lucid by morning."

Figuring. If I leave right now, I have a shot at making the midnight flight. "Doc. I've got to get off the phone."

"Oh . . . there was one more thing."

"Yeah?"

"Happy birthday."

3

Flying. Early early morning. A sheet of gray clouds rolls to the horizon. Already, strips of white are streaking across their faces as the sun begins oozing over the top. Thirty thousand feet. What shoe salesmen dream of. Write it down. I take out the spiral notebook. No, too stupid.

I love flying. Somehow, it seems like taking a time-out from life. If I'm not actually on the earth, why should I worry about any problems I might have there?

The guy in the aisle seat is complaining to the one in the middle that he has to get a connecting flight in Chicago to New York.

"Do you believe it, six hours just to fly to New York? That's a long time to be on a plane." The guy in the middle nods affirmatively but turns his head away slightly as he does so. The message is clear. Shut up!

Somewhere in a history book, I remember reading that it took the settlers nearly a year to make the
trip cross country in a covered wagon. In another
hundred years, it'll probably take six minutes. "Good
God, six minutes. That's a long time to take just to
cross the country." Put it in the notebook? Why not,
I can always cross it out later.

My back is killing me. Too much sitting. I'm at
that age where my back gets stiff, my knees get stiff
. . . everything but what I want gets stiff. Write it
down. Keep thinking about it. Maybe some other lines
there.

"Doctors don't know anything about backs. The
last one I went to told me I should sleep with a pillow
between my knees. So I did. Oddly enough, it really
helped my back . . . but I just about broke my neck
keeping my head on that pillow." Write it down.

This is a perfect bit for Robertson if the jerk can
force himself to pause.

The seat is simply too small for comfort. Start
writing again. "Airplanes are designed for midgets, I
swear. Tiny little seats, itty-bitty pillows, and teeny-
weeny food. The only thing that's adult-size is the air
fare.

"Nowadays, you can tell what city you're going
to even before you get there. 'Las Vegas,' the pilot
announces, 'I'm giving eight-to-three odds I can land
on one wheel.' 'L.A.,' the pilot says. 'We're . . . like
. . . approaching the airport and . . . like . . . we'll
probably land . . . but, you know . . . I'm a Sagittar-
ius so, I . . . like . . . you know . . . might change my
mind . . .' "

Another piece: "The difference between living
in the Midwest and living in L.A. In the Midwest, you
put chains around your tires, not your neck."

Back to the airplane bit: "On a New York flight,
when you ask the attendant for coffee, she either

ignores you or starts yelling for a cop. On the way to Chicago, when you ask the flight attendant for coffee, she replies, 'Make me.' "

I scribble *Airplane* at the top of the page and close the spiral notebook. Glancing at my watch. We're about thirty minutes away from landing. Already, the plane is beginning its glide back toward earth.

If I were a plane, I'd never want to land. In the air, majestic. Flip your wings and you go singing across the sky. But from the moment you brake on the runway, you're an oaf. Can't even back up on your own. A tiny little truck has to push you away from the gate. How embarrassing.

Most people have been sleeping during the flight. A mother and her child walk by. He looks exactly like Billy Metzer. I wonder if she'd mind if I punched his lights out.

I'm ten and Danny's seven. Billy Metzer, the neighborhood bully with the body of a man, the age of a boy, and the brains of a tomato. He is so big that he wears his desk around his hips. Billy Metzer is built like a predator. Ninety percent of his body weight is in his fists. You could never say to Billy Metzer, "Why don't you pick on somebody your own size?" because most fathers in the neighborhood aren't into fighting ten-year-olds.

At that age, however, my body is an evolutionary contradiction. Most of me wants to survive, which is why my legs stop just below my neck. But the rest of me is all mouth, which is the part that seems determined to make all of me extinct.

Standing around the playground after school. A lot of the fights happen on the playground. You have to be in good shape to fight in my neighborhood because you have to walk around in circles for hours.

Usually, a lot more words are thrown than punches.

"Make me."

"No, you make me."

"I dare you."

"I double-dare you."

"Double-darers go first."

"I'm rubber, you're glue. Everything you say bounces off me and sticks to you."

I don't think the neighborhood ever produced a fighter. But I bet it produced a ton of lawyers.

Billy Metzer is different from most of us kids. He really likes to fight. When there aren't any other kids around, Billy Metzer picks fights with trees and wins.

Danny's with me. It's been one of those days when he has followed me everywhere I've gone. That kind of stuff drives me nuts.

Even though he's three years younger, Danny is already almost as tall as me and he weighs more than I do.

We see Billy Metzer menacing his way through the crowd. Metzer zeroes in on Danny. Too late, I realize that Danny's a perfect target. For one thing, he's about as aggressive as a gerbil.

Metzer bullies up to Danny. "You know what, Cooper, my old man's the toughest guy in the neighborhood."

Although the statement is aimed specifically at Danny, it's designed to insult all of us. Metzer is basically saying that our fathers are wimps. An insult that ten-year-olds do not take lightly. On the other hand, most of us would like to live out the afternoon.

Two choices: stand up and be counted—and killed—or slither inside like a worm in a rainstorm. Only two choices. That's it.

Before Danny has a chance to say anything my

mouth takes the third choice. Since Metzer has called my brother by his last name, I just act like he's talking to me instead.

"Metzer, your father isn't the toughest guy in the neighborhood."

We are all stunned, including me. My mouth has always moved faster than my brain. I am hardly the leading candidate to risk my life defending my father's honor. But after the initial shock, smiles appear on everyone's faces. Metzer now has a reason to kill me. Nazis always like to have a reason. "Well, your honor, he looked at me the wrong way." Something. The others can now get their minds off their own cowardice by watching me get destroyed.

Billy Metzer turns toward me. "You saying my father ain't the toughest guy in the neighborhood?"

"You forgot about your mother."

After delivering a line, you always have to take a beat. Onstage, this is known as good timing. On the playground, it's known as suicide. I turn and start to run. Metzer's punch lands on the back of my head. My first memorable one-liner. My first payment.

I go sprawling but my legs never stop churning. I am up and moving again. Metzer proceeds to chase me around the playground and then through half of the neighborhood. But his pursuit is futile and he knows it. A law of the playground: For distances beyond a few inches, feet are faster than fists.

As I'm sprinting down a street, I look over my shoulder and see that Billy Metzer has finally given up. His massive face is soaked with sweat and he's waving his fist at me. "I'll get you, Cooper. If it takes me a hundred years, I'll get you."

To this day, every now and then, I glance over my shoulder, looking for Billy Metzer.

When I get home, Danny is sitting in front of the

television eating a peanut-butter-and-jelly sandwich. I wait for him to say something. Nothing. Finally, I say to him, "Aren't you even going to thank me for saving you from Billy Metzer?"

"What are you talking about?"

"He was about to knock your head off."

"No, he wasn't. He was just telling me how much he admired his father, that's all."

"God," I say, "you are so stupid."

"I'm stupid?" Danny says, "I'm not the one who got punched in the back of the head."

A moment later, he is wrong.

In the next few moments, the plane feathers through the clouds, into that limbo between earth and sky. It lumbers out over Lake Michigan and then angles back as it prepares to land at O'Hare field.

I look at my watch. 5:00 A.M. Below I see Lake Shore Drive. I've driven it hundreds, if not thousands, of times. But now I choose to remember only one. The one at 5:00 A.M.

I'm twenty-one and Danny's eighteen. We have spent the early part of the evening helping Linda Caldwell, a girl from the neighborhood, move to her new high-rise apartment overlooking the lake. Actually, it's four buildings behind the one that overlooks the lake. But from Linda's bathroom window you can see a sliver of blue.

The move has been easy. Linda only had three pieces of furniture, some clothes, and about a dozen cardboard boxes.

Linda is one of the first of our generation to move out of the neighborhood and get an apartment. We three have spent the evening and the early morning hours sitting on her balcony, staring at the city lights, shooting the bull and being totally awed by the world of "Out of school, have a job, and got my own place now."

Linda has faded first, falling asleep just before daybreak. Danny decides to make breakfast—a huge, whatever-you-can-find-throw-it-in omelet. Then he slices up a few potatoes and fries them up with some bacon. Danny cooks. I clean up. That's the way it always is.

Last Sunday morning, when Rita and I had gone out to eat and I ordered that kind of breakfast, she had really gotten worked up over it.

"How can you eat such disgusting food? Just look at all that grease and fat. You're probably going to have a heart attack before you leave the table," she had said.

"If you don't calm down," I replied, "you're going to have one. Besides," I said, "I don't eat this kind of food all the time, but every now and then I enjoy it."

"It's poison."

"It's the all-American breakfast," I said.

"Do you know why it's called 'the all-American breakfast'?" she had asked.

"An act of Congress?"

"No," snapped Rita. "A hundred years ago, this was an agrarian society. For breakfast, people would eat whatever was most convenient. They could get bacon and eggs right from their own livestock."

"I'm glad my great-grandfather never invited me over for breakfast. He had a peat farm."

"It hasn't made any difference," said Rita. "You're still full of it."

After breakfast, Danny and I begin the drive back to the neighborhood in The Fortune. Skimming along

Lake Shore Drive. The sun is just springing up from the bottom of the lake, the radio is playing the right songs, the top is down, and the car, like us, is young and foolish. A little later in the day, it will be too hot. These hours are the filet.

Danny and I are smoking cigars, something that neither of us ordinarily does. But they have become a tradition. Our way of telling each other that life is, indeed, grand.

We are talking about girls. Danny always has "meaningful relationships." I say to him, "In other words, when you meet a girl, you immediately see that she is thoughtful, considerate, intelligent, and that you have a million things in common. It's only a few months later that you notice she has a gorgeous face and a great chest."

Danny just smiles. Ordinarily, I would have found that frustrating. If someone says something, you always have a chance of topping them. But you can't top a smile. Certainly not Danny's. But this morning, we are both too mellow to joust. I just smile, too.

To get home, we have to go through at least a dozen traffic lights. We're in no rush so, naturally, we never catch a red. Getting out of the car in front of the house, I start to say it, but Danny beats me to it.

"How do yellow lights know when you're in a hurry?" An inside joke.

The plane is now only a few moments from touching down. Over one edge of the wing I can see Simone Hospital, where Ma is, and over the other edge, Evergreen Cemetery. The beginning and ending of a life, all within the width of a wing.

A few rays of sunshine have slipped beneath the cloud cover, coloring the autumn leaves. Although

I'm still in the plane, my imagination is already reveling in the cold brashness of the midwestern October air. A welcome relief from the last few days of that almost searing sauna of L.A.

Riding the cab through the streets of Chicago. Reaching for my pack of cigarettes before I remember that I've only got two in my shirt pocket, for emergencies. Even though it isn't even 6:00 A.M. yet, the first wave of early-morning traffic is already beginning to build. Fortunately, Simone Hospital is located only about a mile out of downtown Chicago.

In the past twenty years, I have been back to the city dozens of times but I have always managed to stay in the downtown or near north areas and away from the South Side.

Windier and colder than I thought it would be. A sarcastic day. In Chicago, it's not unusual for winter to make a few guest appearances in the fall.

Trying not to think about Ma but thinking about her anyway.

Five years old. I just can't learn to tie my shoes. In a moment of frustration, Ma says to me, "I don't think you're ever going to learn this."

That night, I dream that I grow up and become President. As I walk down the hall, past two guys, I overhear them talking about me.

"Oh, he's a great president, all right," says one of them, "but you know, the man can't tie his own shoes. He stops by his mother's house every morning on the way into the White House."

The other one nods sadly. "You can always tell when she's out of town. He wears loafers."

Getting out of the cab, paying my fare. As I walk into Simone Hospital, a young woman in a wheelchair holding an infant is being wheeled out by a nurse. Two older women and a young man walk behind. Each of them is loaded down with bouquets of flowers, plants, balloons, and satchels whose side pockets are saddled with baby bottles.

Remembering how it felt, the first time, holding Brian in my arms. Feeling an intensity of love I had never known existed. For an instant, experiencing total terror at the thought of losing him. For the first time, realizing how my parents felt about me.

Hospital visits. Beginnings and endings with a few pit stops in between. Thinking about the biopsy. Wondering if I'm entering the final laps.

Riding up the elevator to the fifth floor. Going to the main desk and asking for Dr. Logan to be paged. The nurse tells me to wait in the solarium, which is at the end of the hall.

I once dated a nurse who worked in a hospital, in the maternity ward. Took her to a party. She bragged to everyone that, in seven years, she had never had a baby on a gurney. She didn't bother telling anyone she was a nurse.

Walking down the corridor, thinking about the results of the lung biopsy. Taking out the spiral notebook. "The last time I was in the hospital, they made me wear one of those gowns that open in the back. Terrific. Now I had a good shot at dying of embarrassment." "And the food . . . the first time they served me lunch I thought my tongue had died." "With medical costs skyrocketing, everyone's trying to cut corners. At my hospital, the diagnostic center now consists of a secretary, a cafeteria employee, and a janitor. All of them claim they're great guessers." "I said to a nurse, 'Can you get a doctor?' She said, 'I think with a different hair style I could.' "

Sitting in the solarium waiting for Dr. Logan to

answer his page. There are a few things I had forgotten to ask him during our brief phone call. I want to make sure I know exactly what the score is before I go in and talk to Ma.

The only other people in the room are a group of middle-aged adults, standing and sitting almost in a huddle. I presume they are brothers and sisters, husbands and wives. They speak in hushed tones.

"She seems more worried about us than herself . . ."

". . . looks so yellow . . ."

". . . She pretends she's asleep when we come in. . . . I think she's embarrassed to have us see her that way. . . ."

"You know, I think she was saying good-bye. . . ."

No huddles for me.

One of them has brought up a plate of spaghetti from the cafeteria and is sprinkling grated cheese on it. I have always detested the odor of grated cheese.

I am sixteen. Danny's thirteen. Lying in our beds late at night. Neither of us is tired even though the clock says we should be. "One of the annoying things about getting older," says Danny, "is that you have to pretend a lot of things aren't true even though you know they are."

"Like what?" I ask.

"Oh, that grated cheese smells like somebody threw up."

We both laugh.

"Or how about," I say, "when you're asked about a letter toward the end of the alphabet, you have to silently say the whole alphabet before you know exactly where it is." Before Danny can reply, I fire in another one. "You never know the great sneaks."

"When you're eating watermelon," says Danny,

"suddenly it's socially acceptable to spit out half your food."

"It's stupid to memorize stuff you can look up in a book."

The pauses between our comments grows with our drowsiness.

"When you really think about it," says Danny sleepily, "eating an egg is disgusting."

"It should be illegal to name someone Fanny."

As I drift off to sleep, I hear Danny mumble, "When Ma's driving you somewhere, how do yellow lights know when you're in a hurry?"

My final shot. "Last week when Ma cooked liver, I walked into the house and the first thing I thought was, Gee, I didn't even know we owned a dog."

Nearly thirty years later, thinking of another one. "Why do bare feet always find broken glass before your eyes do?" Timing is everything, whether it's a second or thirty years.

Dr. Logan, a small, unassuming man, walks in and introduces himself. "There was really no need for you to come so soon, Mr. Cooper," he says. "Your mother told me again this morning that she has plenty of people to look after her—cousins, in-laws, neighbors of course, you are her only son. . . ."

"How is she?"

"Very well. She's taken a bad fall, some bruises, the broken hip, of course, but outside of that . . ."

"Do you know where she fell?"

"You have a small porch on the back of the house?"

"Yes."

"That's where she fell. It was only a few steps, which leads me to suspect that the hip just gave way. A neighbor saw her fall so she got help right away."

I think about how different the scenario might

have been if Ma had fallen down a flight of stairs inside the house.

"Doc, how long will it be before my mother can walk stairs?"

"Stairs? Well, if we're talking two, three steps, I'd say . . . six months. But that's only a guess. It certainly wouldn't be much sooner than that."

"How about more steps than that?"

"How many more?"

"I don't know. Ten or twelve. Stairs to the second floor. Stairs to the basement."

"That many? I really couldn't tell you at this point."

"A long time . . . maybe never?"

"A long time. I really can't be any more specific than that. But, overall, your mother's doing just fine."

Thinking. Fine? No steps? You know what that means? You know what I have to tell her?

"Doc, I appreciate your time. Do you remember what room my mother's in?"

"Twelve thirty-eight." His beeper goes off. Without another word, he turns and walks away.

Taking out the spiral notebook and scribbling. "Doctors are getting sued so much these days that it's becoming impossible to get a straight answer from them. Try and ask one what time it is.

" 'Well, in my professional opinion, it is two-oh-five P.M. But I wouldn't want to be held to that and I would strongly suggest you get a second, and perhaps even a third opinion. You have to realize that there is so much we simply do not know about time. But we do strongly suspect it's a condition that is constantly changing.' "

Remembering the joke I'd heard recently, one that's good enough to steal, about health nuts. "In

forty years, aren't they all going to feel sort of foolish, lying around the hospital, dying of nothing?''

Walking down the hall toward Ma's room. Actually, I'm sort of slithering along the wall. Since I'm
still in view of the nurses' station, I'm hoping I can
slip into her room without anyone noticing.

Ma's the world's worst patient. Dad was just the
opposite. When he was in the hospital, you'd just
about have to put bleachers up in the room to handle
the crowd. It was one long party.

The nurses loved him, too. When the administra-
tion tried to enforce the two-visitors-to-a-patient pol-
icy, the head nurse defined ''visitor'' as anyone
actually sitting on Dad's bed.

Not Ma. The last time I visited her, a nurse
stopped me in the hall and asked me who I was visiting. I gave her a false name.

The only time I was in the hospital, I discovered
I was Ma. On my last night, a nurse came in to change
my bed. I said, ''I bet the nurses are going to be happy
to hear I've been released.''

She replied, ''They'd be happier if they heard
you had died.''

Standing by Ma's door. The television is on. She's
watching her favorite television show, ''Jeopardy.''
I yell around the corner. ''The answer is, a loving son
who flies halfway across the country to see his
clumsy mother.''

Ma laughs and replies. ''Who is Donald Cooper?''

I spring through the door. ''Ta-da. Ma, you're
looking great.''

Leaning over the bed and kissing her. In truth,
although it's only been six weeks since I've seen her
in L.A., she looks ten years older and she seems more
fragile than I would have ever imagined.

''Happy birthday, honey.''

"Thanks, Ma."

"I'm a little embarrassed. I didn't think I'd be seeing you until next month so I haven't bought your gift yet."

"Ma, don't worry about it. Where is everybody?"

"Who?"

"I don't know. Aunt Mary . . . the neighbors, cousin . . ."

"They're all coming this afternoon. Everyone had something to do this morning. Besides, they knew you'd be here."

"How? I wasn't sure I'd be here."

Ma waves her hand to affirm her words. "They knew."

"So, Ma, how come you threw yourself down the stairs?"

"I felt I needed a hobby."

"Seriously, how are you feeling?"

"Very sore. Very, very tired. I hope I don't have to use a walker."

"Not if you don't want to."

Ma says, "You know what I've been thinking about this morning, just before you came in?"

"No, Ma."

"That typewriter your father and I were going to get Danny for his nineteenth birthday. We were going to buy it for him the year before, but the money was a little tight and we just thought . . ."

"Ma, that was so long ago. It doesn't make any difference anymore."

"I know. Still, it bothers me . . ."

Time to change the subject. "How are you doing on 'Jeopardy' this morning?"

Ma says, "Decent, only decent. I watched a little of 'Oprah.' It always amazes me that people get on national television and talk about the most intimate details of their lives. Don't they have any friends . . . any family?''

"I don't know, Ma."

"Last week, I'm taking the bus to Sears, this woman sitting next to me, a perfect stranger—well, she wasn't perfect at all, which is the point—starts telling me about the problems she's having with her husband. I don't want to hear that sort of thing. I listened because that was the polite thing to do. 'Oprah.' Why do people do that? Now, I wouldn't mind going on 'Jeopardy' and showing people how smart I am.''

Ma laughs.

Actually, Ma is pretty smart.

I try to think of something else to talk about, but then decide I might as well get it over with.

"Ma, the doc says you can't go up stairs. You're going to have to sell the house. Look, I can get a great apartment for you out in L.A., just a few blocks away from me. If you don't want to deal with the hassle of an apartment, there's a couple of great retirement centers right near me, too.''

"No.''

"No, what?''

Ma turns up the volume on 'Jeopardy.' "This is my favorite show and you're making me miss it.''

"Ma, you're not listening to me. You can't climb steps. The bathroom's on the second floor. You couldn't go into the basement. You might even have trouble getting out of the house. If you took another fall, it could be very big trouble.

"Look, you've been spending half the year with me in L.A. anyway. Instead of just having a motel room for a couple of months at a time, you can have your own place out there.''

"So fine. If I'm a burden, you don't have to bother having me come out."

"I'm not complaining. How many times have I asked you to move out there? Ma, you know it's time."

Ma turns up the volume again. I just plop down in a chair and wait until "Jeopardy" is over. The second it is, I jump up and start in again.

God, does she give me an argument. The thing is, Ma's the one in the family with common sense. Finally, I say to her, "Ma, listen . . ."

She turns up the volume on the television.

"Listen to me. Remember when I was in high school and I tried out for the varsity baseball team and I didn't make it? God, I was so depressed. You sat down at the kitchen table and began to talk to me—do you remember that?"

Ma turns off the television. "Yes, I remember."

"You tried to cheer me up and I said to you, 'Vince Lombardi says, "Winning isn't everything, it's the only thing." ' And you said to me, in a voice so soft I had to listen, 'Winning isn't anything. You can live an entire lifetime and never win, so it can't be that important. But losing is as much a part of life as breathing.'

"You said to me, 'You're going to lose lots of tryouts. Live long enough, you're going to lose jobs . . . and friends . . . and family. And dreams. Losing, and learning to go on and live again, is the only kind of winning that truly matters.' "

Ma says nothing. She simply stares at the lifeless television.

"Didn't think I remembered all that, huh? You'd be surprised at what I remember."

I walk to the end of her bed and try to get her to look at me. "Ma, you know it's time."

She still won't look at me. No matter. I can see in her eyes that she now realizes this part of her life, the house where she raised her family, the neighborhood where she grew up, met my dad, got married—this part of her life is over. She won't be going home again.

Gently patting her feet beneath the blankets. "Ma, I've got to catch a flight back to L.A. later today but I'll check out apartments and I'll be back in a few days to—"

Ma looks directly at me. "You're not going anywhere until you bring me the brown box."

"Brown box? What brown box?"

"You know."

"No, I don't know. . . . Oh, God, I forgot all about it. . . . Ma, I don't have time."

"I want you to bring that box to me. I want to know that it's safe."

"Why can't Aunt Claire get it?"

"I don't want her snooping around the house."

"Well," I said, "I can understand that." I know Aunt Claire. "But what about one of the neighbors or cousin Eileen?"

"I don't want anyone looking around our house but one of us."

Thinking, Our house. As if I had moved out yesterday.

"Ma, I can't go back to that house . . . I'm never going back . . ."

"In other words . . ." she began.

"Ma, I love you dearly, but I'm never going back."

Ma says, "Never say never."

"You're right, Ma. You're always right. But I'm not going back to that house."

"Donald, for twenty years you've refused to

come home. During all that time, I've never asked
you. But don't you think there were many, many
times I wanted to? Family gatherings, holidays . . .''

"Ma, haven't I flown you out to L.A. anytime
you've said the word? Haven't I—''

"You've been more than generous. But my home
isn't in Los Angeles. Your home isn't . . .''

"Ma . . .''

"I want no one else looking for that box or
touching it.''

"But, Ma . . .''

She turns the television back on.

I walk over and look out the window. All that
looks back is another wing of the hospital. Turning
back to Ma. "Do you know exactly where the box is?
That way I could just run in and . . .''

Ma turns the volume down on the television.
"It's in the back of the guest closet in the living
room.''

"Are you sure?''

"No.''

Glancing at my watch. The flights aren't a problem. There are a few late this afternoon and there
are even a couple tonight. Walking over and kissing
Ma on the head. "I'll see you in a little while.''

"Call me when you get there.''

"Okay.''

"Do you have the number here?''

"Ah . . . no.''

"It's . . .'' she began.

"I don't have anything to write it down on.''

"What about the notebook under your arm?''

"Oh, yeah.'' God, am I absentminded.

Ma gives me the number and I begin walking toward the door.

"You don't have a key,'' Ma says.

"Oh, yeah."

"It's in my coat pocket, which is hanging in the closet."

I open the closet and see the black cloth coat with the tired leather trimming. I remember the Christmas Ma got it. Dad, Danny, and I had bought it for her. Reaching into the pocket and getting the key. It is on a small gold chain. Just one key. I hold it up.

"Is this it?"

"Yes," Ma says.

I start for the door again.

"Donald, you didn't drive here, did you?"

"Funny, Ma."

A family joke. An old one. When I am sixteen and first begin driving, I take the car to church one Sunday morning. Afterward, I walk in the house as Ma is going out. A moment later she's back at the door asking me, "Where's the car?"

"How would I know?"

She says to me, "Because you took it to church."

I had forgotten. I was so accustomed to walking that I had driven to church and then walked home.

As I begin to leave Ma's room, I say to her, "See you in a while, Ma. Ma, the answer is 'Can deliver more guilt per minute than any other mother in the world.'"

The volume jumps up on the television again. "That's a tough one. I'll have to give it some thought."

Standing on a crowded elevator. Right in front of me is a little old man wearing a fedora. Nineteen-fifties—right in style. During those years, either the hat's grown or his head has shrunk. Now, the hat sits down around his ears.

All of us are watching the numbers go by. A young man gets on. It's one of these elevators where when you press the number you want, the little square lights up. The only one presently lit up is *One*. He hesitates and then presses *One* again. As if the rest of us hadn't done it right.

That kind of stuff's annoying, not annoying in a big way but annoying just the same. I feel like saying, "Oh, thank you, sir, thank you thank you thank you. If you hadn't gotten on this elevator, God only knows where all of us would have ended up." That's what I feel like saying, but not enough to say it.

Jumping into a cab. Thirty minutes later, we're going by Carl's Service Station, which is only two miles from the neighborhood. We're getting close.

4

I'm nineteen and Danny's sixteen. We stop there at Carl's one night for gas. Danny's driving. He asks for five dollars' worth of gas. After it's pumped, he discovers he only has two bucks.

Carl, who's one of the owners, is enraged. Danny offers to leave the car, and me, as collateral, and walk the four miles back and forth to our house for the money. That calms down Carl. By the time we leave, Carl has told Danny to fill it up and pay him when he has the chance.

Danny becomes a regular customer. Carl becomes a lifelong friend. If the situation had depended on my charm, we would have gone to jail.

The cab stops at a traffic light. On the corner is a sporting-goods store. Its face reflects the time of the year. Footballs are sitting in the corners of the dis-

play window while jerseys of the Chicago Bears are
pinned against the back wall.

Watching a game last Sunday afternoon, I realized how your age can affect your view of pro football. When I was young, I would have loved to have
done it. When I got a little older, I wondered how
they did it. Now I wonder why.

I am twenty and Danny's seventeen. Only a few
weeks after his high school graduation. One night in
early summer, a group of my buddies and Danny, too,
go to the park to play some touch football. The only
light on the field comes from street lamps scattered
symmetrically throughout the park.

Danny and I are sitting on the ground putting on
our spikes. A few of the guys are already throwing
the football around while a couple of others are
standing on the edge of the field, laughing about
something. One of the guys, like Danny and me, is
still changing shoes.

"I love this kind of stuff," I say. "Playing football with the guys."

"This is it," says Danny unenthusiastically.

"That's what I said."

"What I mean," says Danny slowly, "is that this
is probably one of the last times you guys will ever
get together like this."

"What are you talking about? We've been hanging around with each other since we were kids."

"You're not kids anymore."

"Get to the point," I say. Danny can sure be a
pain in the ass.

"On our way over here," Danny says, "you were
telling me how long it had been since you guys have
gotten together."

"So?" I snap.

"You told me you never see Anderson anymore. Miller's not here . . ."

"Miller joined the marines," I say.

"Whatever." Danny gestures toward a few of the guys. "Parker's getting married . . . Smith and Kuzinski both go away to school so they're only home for the summers, and usually they go back early. Malecki has a bad back so he doesn't play anymore. I'll be starting college myself."

"Yeah," I say sharply, "and I'll be working more nights at the shoe store." .

"I didn't mean it that way."

"Uh-huh." I know he didn't, but it ticks me off anyway.

My shoelace snaps. "Damn it. You got an extra one?"

"No." Danny looks down at my shoe. "But there's still enough to tie it."

"I guess so," I say.

"Ever take pictures with your mind?" asks Danny.

"I have no idea what the hell you're talking about."

"You know," says Danny. He forms a square with his index fingers and thumbs and then pushes down with one of the index fingers as he makes clicking sounds. "You look around and you try to visualize exactly what this moment is like so you'll remember it the rest of your life."

Standing up and feeling the spikes bite into the ground. "You're strange, you know that?"

"I was just saying—"

"No need to remember tonight. There will be plenty of others just like this one," I say.

Spikes make me feel like I can run forever but I settle for thirty or forty yards as I sprint across the grass. Pausing a moment to catch my breath. Looking back across the field. Danny is just getting to his feet. One of the guys tosses him the football. Strings of light drift in from the distant street lamps and limp across the field.

Danny is right. I see Warren Marker and Paul Godding a few more times but not on a football field. I never see any of the others again. But I still have the pictures.

A few minutes later, I'm standing on a corner only three blocks away from the house where I grew up. Of course, I could have had the cab drop me right off in front of the house but, well, at the park swimming pool, no matter how cold the water was, a lot of the other kids, including Danny, would jump right in. Not me. I always started with just the big toe.

Those summer swimming lessons. I had to take them every year from the time I was eight until I was twelve. Danny went with me the first summer. He didn't have to go after that.

The water at the park swimming pool was so cold it couldn't freeze. Our collective shivers sent waves through the pool.

On the first day, there would be fifty "Guppies." A month later, at the graduation ceremonies, forty-nine "Whales" would swim on and only one Guppy would remain behind. By the time I gave up on the swimming lessons, Danny had become an expert diver. Big deal. We were both ending up on the bottom of the pool.

Looking around at this neighborhood. People talk about going back to "the old country." This is "the old country" for me. I can't trace my family's history any further back than my grandparents.

My father was from a family of fifteen children. My grandfather was a sports fan. His favorite sport

was my grandmother. My dad's joke. I miss his sense
of humor.

Walking. Taking my time. Sooner or later, everybody comes back. One day, they may drive a few
blocks out of their way to go down its streets or, like
me, their memories bring them back here time after
time.

In the summer, there was a little old man with
an ice cream truck. Hated kids. Used to drive down
the streets at ninety miles an hour.

It's cold but the sky has cleared up. Damn, I
didn't even think to bring a jacket. An autumn sun.
When I walk in the shade, I get chills.

Glancing at my watch. It's a little after 8:00 A.M.
Most of the men have already left for work. I notice
a lot of women walking to the bus stop. Kids are on
their way to school. There don't seem to be as many
as I remember.

When I was growing up here, there were billions
of us. It was the kind of neighborhood that when
parents had an accident they raised it. Only middle
children could be reasonably certain they were "chosen." I had at least two friends who discovered they
had been conceived because their parents had gone
to a wedding reception and had drunk a bit too much.
This getting born business can be tricky.

When I was a kid, I couldn't wait to get out of
here. I don't know why. I guess it's like the chicken
inside the egg. The reason isn't so important. It's the
getting out that is.

But now these streets seem cozier than any I've
walked in a long, long time.

This neighborhood is like a small town. You drive
down the street, people you don't even know will
wave at you. Of course, in L.A. strangers will wave
at you, too. They just won't use all their fingers.

This is a neighborhood. It's not a "development"

or a "project" or a "subdivision" or a "community village." It's a neighborhood. The trees are taller than the kids. The corner store's on the corner and the garages are in the alleys where they should be. This is a neighborhood.

You never saw a squad car around here. If you did something wrong, why would somebody call a cop if they knew your mother? A cop can only shoot you. Your mother can always nag you to death.

The houses are neighborhood houses. You almost never find a stucco house around here. They belong in California, where everything's stucco, including your friends.

There are a fair number of Cape Cods on these blocks. I wouldn't want to live in a house built by someone who couldn't tell the difference between the Midwest and New England. The top floor of a Cape Cod, which is more commonly known as an attic in other houses, is always the childrens' bedroom. Kids who grow up in Cape Cods have peculiar angles to their heads.

Or ranch houses. Where's the ranch? Just because it takes the back end of a horse to buy one doesn't make it a ranch house.

This neighborhood has real houses, like the Chicago bungalow. With walls about forty feet thick, it's built to last slightly longer than eternity. Scientists will tell you that from outer space the only two man-made things that can be seen are the Great Wall of China and the Chicago bungalow. That's what they'll tell you.

Then there's the Chicago two-flat, known to the rest of the world as simply a two-story apartment building. Designed so that three generations can live in the same building. Isn't that wonderful?

When Sis gets married, she can move upstairs. Good-bye rent money. When she starts having kids, she can move downstairs and Mom and Dad can move upstairs. Little brother, that swinging bachelor, can have his own pad in the basement. Three kids? That's what garages are for. Four? Hey, Mom and Dad can't live forever.

I grew up in a Georgian, a house that looks like it was designed after the box the basketball came in.

The lawns around here are small. Good trick-or-treating territory. In some of those suburbs, the lots are so wide that you waste most of the night just getting across them. The great houses gave out full sized candy bars, not those little ones that companies make just for Halloween. The weirdos gave out fruit. Trying to make Halloween an exercise in health. That's sick.

I am twelve years old and Danny is nine. Twelve years old is prime time for a trick-or-treater. You're old enough to stay out until nine but still young enough that you don't feel like a fool wearing a costume and standing at somebody's door asking for candy.

But that afternoon, I come down with a fever. I can't believe it. All the times I had faked being sick to stay home from school and now I really am.

Sitting in the living room watching Danny getting ready to leave. I can't remember what kind of costume he was wearing. Usually, on this night, he was a major drag on me, tagging along until he had to go in at seven-thirty. This was the first year that Ma was allowing him to stay out until eight-thirty.

That morning, I had warned Danny, "No way you're gonna tag along with me and my friends all night, no way."

He had said, "Don't worry. I have my own friends. I can take care of myself."

Now he was.

Watching him walk out the door with his shopping bag. Whatever he is wearing, it is dangling around his feet. Ma has to tell him twice to pick it up. All his friends are waiting on the porch.

Feeling the frustration of missing the chance of a lifetime. You only get one Halloween a year and you only get one "twelve." I can't even answer the door for other trick-or-treaters. Ma is afraid of the dreaded "draft."

Danny is back at seven-thirty. At first, I presume he has just come in to use the bathroom or get another bag. But no, he sits down on the floor, in front of the couch where I'm lying, and announces he's had enough. I'm a little surprised but Ma isn't. Danny's always doing dumb things.

He gets ready to dump his bag of candy onto the floor. Taking inventory is part of the ritual. I figure he'll give me a few pieces of candy. That's the way Danny is. When he pours out the candy, I see that there is two of everything.

"I told everybody," Danny says, "that I had a sick brother at home."

The amazing part is everyone believed him.

Walking by Ray Ratsen's house. You could become a neighborhood legend just by doing one stupid thing of epic proportions. Ratsen was a legend many times over. He once drove his car through the front window of a snack shop just to deliver the one-liner, "But the sign says you have a drive-up window." Ratsen had a problem with alcohol. He couldn't get enough of it.

Opening the spiral notebook and jotting that down. Spellito loves drinking jokes. Maybe he can try it at that showcase in Vegas he's doing next week.

Bobby Capello's house. His childhood dream was

to drive a train. A few years ago, Ma told me that he had been made a vice-president of a major railroad. I bet he'd still rather be driving the train. Kids have an instinct for what jobs are really the good ones.

On my block now. But my house is on the same side of the street so I can't see it yet. It was on this very sidewalk that my dad taught me how to ride a bike.

He'd walk me down the sidewalk, one hand fisted around the front bar, right in the center, the other, out of sight, holding on to the back of the seat. I gripped the handlebars as I pretended to steer.

For the most part, I would try to keep my balance, but every now and then I'd shake the bike, just a little, to see if Dad was paying attention. He was.

As my sense of balance grew, the hand on the front of the bike gradually disappeared. The ride was a little shakier but only where his support had once been. In what seemed like a few moments, even that unsteadiness disappeared.

I was riding much better but we both knew who was really in charge. We both knew that if it hadn't been for the unseen hand, there would be no ride at all.

Now, even the unseen hand was letting go, at first just for an instant and, at first, I instantly knew. My dad, sensing the fear, would hesitate and wait as long as possible before regrabbing control as I began to lose my balance.

Although we never talked about it, we were both aware that the other one knew how the game was played. Dad would begin letting go more often, for longer times. Sometimes I knew, sometimes I didn't. But even when there was no hand on the back of the seat, Dad was still there walking along beside me.

My confidence was growing. One day, I got a little careless. The next thing I knew I was on the side-walk and the bike was on top of me. Dad pulled up the bike and patted the seat. Bruised both physically and spiritually, I slowly climbed back up, but I made sure there was a hand holding it steady.

One day, I was riding along . . . I said something . . . and realized Dad wasn't there. Looking over my shoulder, very quickly, I saw him standing on the sidewalk at least six houses away, yelling, "Look ahead, not at me," and so I did. Since then, I've fallen quite a few more times but now I can pick myself up.

Now I'm a dad, too. Thinking of Brian. When do I say something? When do I shut up? Like every father, I know that I cannot walk with my child forever. He'll travel many miles without me. But, like all children, someday he'll look back upon the path he has traveled. He will realize that some dads hang on too long and others not at all. He'll know what kind of job has been done. And really, what else matters?

Danny learned to ride a bike in a slightly different way.

One afternoon, when he's six years old, he asks some kid if he can borrow his bike. I'm playing a few houses away. Danny rides right by me. I yell at him, "Hey, you jerk, you don't know how to ride a two-wheeler." He rides right into a tree. But after that, he did okay.

Walking by Devlins' house. I forgot all about them. Mr. Devlin was a bricklayer. Here, people had jobs you could understand. Today, you ask someone what they do for a living and they'll say something like, "I'm a systems coordinator for nonperishable goods on the Delta computer system."

Yes, but what the hell do you do? People here had jobs that made sense. My dad, he drove a potato chip truck. Makes sense to me. I've seen trucks. I've seen potato chips. Even eaten them. Mr. Kolaski, down the street, he sold shoes. You know, shoes, for your feet.

When people moved here, they came to stay. Shoe salesmen don't get transferred to New York very often. In fact, when a family finally did move, the house kept their name for another ten years. "So, you live in the Millers' house . . ."

Men did not come home from work and jog. Only one guy in the neighborhood "pumped iron" and everybody thought he was crazy. My dad once said, "Lifting weights is like loading a truck that isn't there."

The women? Ask a woman what she did and she'd say she was a housewife. "Just" hadn't gotten into the phrase yet. There were a few working mothers, like Mrs. Kasmas. Her son grew up to be a gangster. The other mothers were delighted.

Mrs. Kendall's house. This was the house we crept by when we were kids. Mrs. Kendall was a "divorced" woman. Not "a" divorced woman, but "the" divorced woman. Years ago, when you walked by, you could see the flames of hell licking up at her door. Well, my mother could.

Back then, people seemed to realize that passion was for the short haul but marriage was for the long haul. Now, one of you burps the wrong way and the other one's hooking up the U-Haul.

I don't realize what a different world Brian is growing up in until I take him to a birthday party when he is three years old. One parent is on their second marriage and the other is on their third. There are six grandparents, two half-brothers, one stepmother, and a guy who is introduced as a former stepfather. The adults outnumber the kids.

When I get back from the party, I tell Melinda about it. We both think it's pretty funny until about two years later when it's our turn.

For a few years, Brian keeps the marriage together or, perhaps, he keeps Melinda and me apart. When Brian is six years old, Melinda says that maybe she and I are seeing too much of each other.

"Melinda," I say, "we're married to each other."

"You know what I mean," she says. "We work in the same office, live in the same house—"

I interject, "Argue with the same people . . ."

Melinda replies that she is seriously thinking about having another child but doesn't want one as old as me.

She takes another job doing the same kind of work but with a different company. One night she comes home and tells me she has fallen in love with another employee.

Fathers are like generals. Even if you're a distance from the action, you can still be one. But it's not the same—being at dinner every evening, getting the news about his day at school. When he gets sick in the middle of the night. Being there when he wakes up in the morning. Hearing about his problems when he wants to talk about them rather than when you have the time to listen.

In a divorce, the father almost always loses in rank, especially when the mother remarries. A part of the father remains but there are other parts now: Part uncle, part very much older brother, part friend, and part stranger, which is, perhaps, why the parts never seem to add up to a whole.

Regardless, I am still Brian's father and I revel in the role. In his terms, perhaps I'm not on center stage, but I'm always one of the major characters.

One morning, when Brian is about four years old, he gets mad at me because I won't allow him to have a candy bar for breakfast. He says, "When I grow up, I'm going to forget you. I'm going to remember Mommy but I'm going to forget you."

I tell him, "You may hate me, you may love me. But you are never going to forget me."

I am an only child until I'm three years old and Danny comes along. Just like that, I go from being the main event to the opening act. I've never really adjusted.

Remembering the day Ma named him. It is a late, hot, muggy summer afternoon, around five o'clock. Ma waddles across the kitchen—she's pregnant and then some. She has told me that I'm going to get a little brother or sister to play with. Looks to me more like I'm going to get two or three of each.

Ma opens the back door. In the distance, you can hear the voices of other mothers calling for their children to come home to dinner. Each voice, a melody of its own. A neighborhood song where the words never rhyme.

Ma shouts, "Danny, oh, Dannnny, supper time. Dannnny!" She smiles, closes the door, and that's it.

The way that Ma would yell out that door, she must have thought we were playing in Wyoming.

I don't remember that much about Danny's young years. Don't remember that much about mine. He crawls a lot. Backward. I have a toy car that does that. One morning, I get so frustrated with it that I stamp on it. When Ma complains about Danny getting underfoot, I suggest the same thing. She doesn't appreciate it.

Early on, Danny demonstrates self-destructive

tendencies. He is not yet three. A family vacation. We have just pulled up to a summer cottage. I have to go to the bathroom so Ma rushes me into the house. Dad is carrying in luggage. He yells to my mother, "Do you think it's all right for Danny to stand outside by himself?"

Ma yells back, "There's nothing out there. It's just an empty field. What could he possibly do?"

Two minutes later, Danny walks into the cottage. Blood is streaming down his face. Apparently, he had thrown a rock up in the air and then stood under it. That's what he could possibly do.

When Danny comes along, I become "older." "Donald, you're older so you should know better." I become "responsible." "Donald, watch Danny. Remember, you're responsible." I become "one of you boys." "Would one of you boys get the butter for me?"

When I was a little kid, I thought my parents knew everything. When I became a big kid, I realized they didn't know anything at all. Now, I know I was right both times.

The truth is, none of us is raised by perfect people. My parents made mistakes, plenty of them. But the sign of becoming an adult, and I'd like to think I am one, is that you look back on your young years, you see what was done right and repeat it. You see what was done wrong and learn from it so that when the next generation comes along you can make your very own mistakes.

My parents had an agreement they would never go to bed mad at each other. Made it kind of tough on us kids. Not easy talking to someone who hasn't slept in fourteen years. Dad's joke.

Ma, a big Ed Sullivan fan. Honest to God. She read somewhere that he had said, "When everything at home's okay, then everything's okay." She liked that.

In my house, there was no such thing as "woman's work," but there was such a thing as "man's work." Ma wouldn't wash walls or cut lawns. That was a man's job. But my dad did dishes, vacuumed, he could cook almost as well as Ma. When you lost a button, you went to my dad, not Ma. He was the one from a family of fifteen.

My parents were a team.

When Danny and I are little kids, my dad gets some kind of infection and is out of work for six months. Ma goes out and gets a job while Dad stays home with us kids. When he gets better, he goes back to the potato chip truck and Ma quits her job. No big deal.

Rubbing my throat. It seems to be getting sorer. It almost feels as if the tube's still in there. My throat hasn't felt this raw since I was seven.

If you're going to get sick, you had better make sure it's Ma who's in charge.

During those six months of Dad's reign, I have a tonsillectomy. My throat is so sore that when I take a sip of water it feels like I've inhaled a blowtorch.

After a couple of days of not eating, I am getting desperate. I ask Dad if there's anything in the house I can eat. At the moment, he's preoccupied with fixing the toilet. Maybe he thinks it's Danny who's asking him. Worst yet, maybe he doesn't. He gives me graham cracker cookies. To this day, I can't look at a gravel road without getting a lump in my throat.

Looking at Warren Marker's house. On the day we graduate from grammar school, Warren, Paul, and I sit on our bikes, on Warren's front sidewalk, our baseball gloves in our hands, as Mrs. Marker takes our picture. How many lives have I lived since then?

Approaching. Stopping and staring. I haven't seen it in over twenty years. All the family history that's important to me happened here, in this neighborhood, in this house.

5

The front porch. I forgot all about it. I mean, I didn't forget that we have a front porch but that we have a "Front Porch."

Where I live now, the houses don't have front porches. Oh, there's a slab of concrete in front of the door and there's a roof over it, but they're not front porches. You never see anyone sitting on them.

In most neighborhoods of the world, this wouldn't even be considered a porch but more of a glorified stoop. But here, it's a porch.

Sitting on the top step, in the center. I swear, I can feel the grooves my rear end has left in the concrete. When I was fourteen years old, here, right here, is where I sat with Donna Trandelli. She had an older sister, so her front porch was always taken.

Donna had to be home by nine o'clock and she couldn't go out on school nights, so late August, when the nights arrive early, were the best. Donna and I would sit here and talk and . . . do the very best you could on a front porch. Her father worked in the steel mills, in the office. Didn't like me.

I was wild about Donna Trandelli. I didn't exactly worship the ground she walked on. But I was very fond of it. I thought she was going to be "the one."

Meeting Melinda. The day after I graduate from college, I moved out to L.A., not so much that I wanted to be there but because I didn't want to be here. Would have gone farther but the water stopped me.

I had met Melinda on a job interview. She was the personnel director. I asked her out for coffee. After a few dates, she offered me a position but no job. I took it. A few months after we started seeing each other, Melinda took a new job writing instruction manuals. She then got me hired to do the same thing. A habit left over from the old job.

I really wasn't sure I wanted the job but Melinda encouraged me to, as she put it, "seize the opportunity." We had already been talking marriage and Melinda had made it clear to me that she didn't think it was a good idea to become permanently involved with someone who was unemployed. Besides, I really needed the money.

But, within a few months, my benign tolerance for the work grew into an intense hatred. Every day, as I labored over those insipid instruction manuals, I waited for the call that never came from Masters and Johnson.

When I complained about the job, Melinda thought I was complaining about her. The irony was that I probably couldn't have operated any of the things for which I was writing the instruction manuals. Usually, I would just take the designers' or the technicians' notes and rewrite them in a language more closely resembling English.

Once I wrote an instruction manual for a new typewriter. The company was so pleased with the job I did they gave me one of their typewriters. I couldn't figure out how to operate it.

Two months after the storm, Melinda realized she was pregnant. Since she was using birth control, I asked her how that could happen. She said she thought she had misread the instructions. She accused me of having written them.

The other thing we used to do on the front porch— not Donna and me. Danny and me. We'd play rubber ball off the steps. Actually, I'd only play with Danny if there was nobody else around. He was three years younger so he wasn't very good.

If any of my buddies came along, even if I was already in a game with Danny, I'd dump him and play with my buddy instead. A lousy thing to do. But then, I could be lousy. Danny would act as if he didn't care but I knew he did.

Ma would get mad. She wouldn't make me play with him, but she'd always say, "Remember, your friends come and go, but you only have one brother." Ma, the guilt queen.

When we played the game, neither player was standing in front of the house. Me, I was in center field, Comiskey Park, in front of fifty thousand fans.

No matter who I was playing with, we might have played eight billion times the day before, we'd still go over the rules. Let's see . . . "If the ball gets past you, but you manage to touch it, then it's a single. If it gets by you clean, a double. If it rolls to the street, a triple, and across the street, a home run.

"If you catch the ball on the fly past the side-walk, it's a double play. If a red Buick's going by, it's a triple play, and if you throw the ball against the door, then we both run like hell." Ma wasn't a base-ball fan.

When I was a little kid, my dad bought me a bag of toy soldiers. I set them up on the lawn so they could watch me play baseball.

Remembering that I had also bought Brian a bag of toy soldiers and he had taken them to his room and put them in neat rows so he could perform be-fore them.

Inside the house, the phone begins ringing. Prob-ably Ma. She said she'd wait for me to call her, but I know Ma. Standing up and searching myself for the key. Damn. Finally, I find it in my back pocket, where I had already checked twice before. But by the time I get the key in the lock, the phone stops ringing.

No problem. Ma will call again. Sitting back down on the front porch. For the first time, I really look at the key Ma has given me.

"The key to the house." When I was a kid, being given a key to the house was a major step in the climb to adulthood. The first time Dad gave me a key, he sat me down at the kitchen table and said, "Son, this is a very big responsibility. I am entrusting the entire safety of our home to you. Being given this key is a sign that you're growing up, you're maturing. You're becoming a man." I was seven.

Dad had a real thing about the key to the house. I could come home and say, "Dad, I went to the store and lost Danny. I have no idea where he is."

"That's okay. He knows his way home."

"And I lost the key to the house."

"Damn it, damn it, damn it."

Even though for years, sporadically, I had a key to the house, I didn't get to use it more than two or three times. The front door was for "company." When I was ten years old, I fell on a piece of glass and sliced open my arm. In my hysteria, I went running to the front door. "Ma, I'm bleeding to death."

"Go to the back door."

You also had to take your shoes off when you walked into the house. This was virtually a universal rule in my neighborhood. We were all Muslims but didn't know it.

When I was out of high school, Dad actually lost his own key to the house. He was frantic. He wanted Ma to change the locks. She said, "What's the point? The lock on the back door's never worked."

Sometimes my dad and I, we'd sit out here and listen to the ball game on the radio. We'd talk to people as they walked by.

In L.A. no one ever just walks by except three-year-olds running away from home and people "exercising."

People around here walk for a different reason; to get from one place to the other.

Not much of a need to sit on front porches anymore. Air-conditioning's had a lot to do with it. Even when Dad and I sat out here, some of these houses already had those window units. Dad said you could always tell which ones did. On hot summer nights, their front porches would be empty.

Anyway, my dad and I, we'd sit out here, we'd stay hello to our neighbors, we'd talk to them. That's how we learned to care about them, and they about us. My dad used to say, "The world would be a better place if there were fewer air conditioners and more front porches."

My dad, a quick temper but basically an easygoing guy. He could only stay mad for a few words at a time. When my dad was with the rest of the family, he was your typical "telling you what to do" father. But when it was just him and me, and I guess it was the same way when he was with Danny, he was a different kind of guy. He was fun.

Some people didn't like my dad and I think that was why. The man just seemed to be having too much fun with his life. After all, the rest of us were alive, too, weren't we? And we weren't having that much fun. So what made him so special?

But looking back, I realize that he loved his job—driving that potato chip truck and delivering those potato chips—and he enjoyed his family. What's left? I guess I've never thought much about it before, but my dad was probably one of the most successful men I've ever known.

But he was the kind of guy who, every now and then, needed to be alone. He obviously couldn't afford to go to the Bahamas for a few weeks. He couldn't even afford to go to a cottage in Michigan for the weekend. So when life got my dad down, he'd go to his favorite vacation spot, the bathroom.

He'd get something to read, like the Encyclopedia Britannica, and he'd go into the bathroom. Now the only thing that would drive my dad over the edge would be if somebody shouted at him through that bathroom door.

As a little kid, I might go up to the door and say, "Ah, Daddy, I can't find my—"

"Damn it, damn it, damn it. Isn't there anywhere a man can sit down without hearing the word *dad?*"

As you got older, you learned the rules but sometimes I'd knock on that door just to annoy the hell out of him.

Eventually, he'd come out—two, three weeks later—a new man. Relaxed. Happy. He'd know everything from *A* to *Z*. He'd even have a tan. It was the strangest thing.

When I was a teenager, I spent a lot of time in the bathroom combing my hair. Trying to get that wave just right. Sometimes Danny would be standing next to me, trying to get his wave just right.

One day he's having a real tough time.

I look down at him and say, "Jerk, that's a crewcut."

I'm eight years old and Danny's five. Ma asks me to take Danny to the barber shop, which is four blocks from here in that direction. A real adult responsibility. When we get there, Donna Trandelli's already there with her little brother.

I'm sitting in the chair, trying to act like an adult, when Danny starts telling these stupid knock-knock jokes and jokes like, "Why wouldn't the banana jump off the Empire State Building? Because it was yellow." That kind of garbage.

Not only are the jokes terrible but he's screwing them all up. Well, he's only five years old. Besides, he's laughing so much you can hardly understand him. Donna thinks he's cute so she laughs at the first joke. Maybe a few other people did, too.

That's all Danny has to hear. He just keeps telling one after the other. He doesn't notice that after the first joke, he's the only one laughing.

Donna starts staring at me as if I'm the nutty one. I felt like such a jerk.

On the way home, Danny's still telling jokes and laughing like a madman. I'm trying to stay angry at him but it's not easy. After a while, just from listening to him cackle, I start laughing, too. Now we're both laughing like madmen. Only eight years old and already I'm discovering that insanity runs in families.

* * *

Sometimes, my dad would sit here on the porch and tinker with something he was trying to fix. That's when Danny would be sitting with him, not me. I hate that kind of stuff.

On many Sunday afternoons, the car would be sitting at the curb, its hood propped open, and Danny and Dad would have the upper half of their bodies immersed in the engine. They'd often extract something and take it back to the front porch where they'd continue to discuss and dissect the slimy pieces of engine they held in their hands.

Danny and Dad seemed to know everything about cars. I'm lucky if I can unlock one. They'd often spend hours talking about cars and other mechanical mysteries just as Danny and I would spend hours talking about sports.

Dad certainly did his best to convert me. When I was ten, he bought me a model aircraft carrier kit, with three thousand pieces, for my birthday. Even then, I knew that the man had things backward. I could certainly take a toy that was in one piece and give it back to him in three thousand pieces. But I could hardly do it the other way around.

When I was twelve, Dad bought me a jigsaw. For one of the rare times in my life, I showed good judgment. I didn't touch the thing until nine years later when I threw it out. If I hadn't shown such insight, I wouldn't have had the arms to throw it out.

Noticing a chip in the concrete on the edge of the second step. If you could throw the ball off this chip, it was a sure triple.

Suddenly remembering. Walking a few houses over to the intersection of 110th and Drake. When I was a little kid, this was the best place in the world to play baseball. This sewer top was home plate. That one's first base . . . second base . . . third.

Where I live in L.A., you could never play baseball in the streets. There are hardly any corners. The
streets sort of swirl around each other. Try playing
baseball and second base could be six blocks away.

The city park is only two blocks from here but
you have to cross a busy street to get there and most
of our mothers wouldn't allow us. Mother logic. You
can't cross a street, but you can play in one.

Actually, what we played here was sixteen-inch
softball, a brand of baseball once found only in Chicago. In the last few years, it's been introduced to a
few other parts of the country by migrating Chica-
goans. But these newly converted have diluted the
purity of the game by wearing gloves. A true sixteen-
inch softball player would sooner wear a dress.

A brand-new sixteen-inch softball is about the
size of a bowling ball but considerably harder. It gets
soft only after a couple of months of use. Playing
with an old sixteen-inch softball is hardly worth the
effort. It has all the excitement of a pillow fight.

Sixteen-inch softball is for kids on street corners
and middle-aged men at the park. It's perfect for
street corners because when you pitch it to a ten-
year-old, it's an even fight.

There wasn't a kid in the neighborhood who
could hit the ball more than forty feet. Windows on
corner houses were almost never threatened by a
sixteen-inch softball. On those rare occasions, when
a sixteen-inch softball was hit hard, it would turn a
street corner game into a pinball machine as it pinged
players racing to get out of its way.

With a sixteen-incher, you could actually hear a
ground ball coming at you. Getting hit with a line
drive was the equivalent of being shot by a cannon.
Fly balls were tricky. If the ball got between you and
the sun, the entire sky would grow dark. The trampoline method was the best way to haul one in. You'd

let the ball bounce off you a few times before you made the final grab.

Most Chicago baseball players quit playing softball when they get old enough to go to the park where the open spaces allow them to play the more traditional size baseball. But by their early twenties, when they start slowing down, many of them return to sixteen-inch, which can also be played at the park.

A sixteen-inch softball player hits his prime in his mid-forties. A good-size beer belly is a major asset. You need all the padding you can get. Sixteen-inchers are notorious for breaking fingers. When an old sixteen-inch softball player folds his hands, it looks like he has a bowl of pretzels in front of him.

Many a Chicagoan has spent virtually every warm evening hour of his life playing sixteen-inch softball. When I was a kid, triple-headers were scheduled at the ballparks with the last game not getting started until after ten o'clock. That was real devotion. The parks didn't have any lights.

Looking over at that big house, the one on the corner. Paul Godding, my best friend, lived there. "Best friend"—that's such an important title when you're a kid.

Paul was a great baseball player. I, on the other hand, was rotten. I was, however, a very fast runner. No matter where a fly ball was hit, I'd always get there just in time . . . to drop it.

Choosing sides. The two biggest guys always chose. One of them was Richie Lapking. In fact, he was not anywhere near being one of the two biggest guys. But no one had the courage to tell him. One guy would toss the bat to the other and, wherever he caught it, they would begin alternately wrapping their fists around it. The last guy to be able to fit his fist on the bat would choose first.

"Okay, I'll take Godding."

"Smith."

"Palkcano."

"Marker," and so on. It always came down to me and Bernard Banterman. Bernard Banterman, who had the body of a bat and a head like a softball.

"Ah . . . I'll take Banterman."

"I guess I've got Cooper then."

"No, we've already got even sides."

"Oh, yeah. That's right. Next time, Cooper."

I'd already be backing away. "Yeah, sure."

Sometimes I'd hang around, especially if it was getting close to dinner. Somebody had to be heading home soon. Sometimes I'd leave. But at those times, there just never seemed to be anyplace to go.

But it was on this street corner that I discovered I loved to play baseball. I absolutely loved it; the feeling of the bat in my hands, that smacking sound when you hit the ball just right. I loved it.

It was right here that I decided what I was going to be, a major-league baseball player. I had everything it took: desire, determination, discipline. The only thing I didn't have was talent. I could always play for the Cubs.

Paul Godding wanted to be a major-league baseball player, too. But, like I told you, he was good. Even Warren Marker, who didn't even care about baseball, the only reason he played was because he hung around with Paul and me, even Warren Marker was better than I was.

Warren wanted to be an artist. He had a box of crayons the size of a small building.

One day, I struck out five times in a row and we were playing slow-pitch. That's like heading to New York and missing it.

I was the only kid to ever do "the home run

trot" on this intersection. When you hit a home run here, it was always of the "run like a lunatic" variety. You couldn't do the "home run trot," because there were, obviously, no fences. But one day, I got to do the "home run trot" anyway, thanks to Richie Lapking.

Richie Lapking was one of the toughest kids in the neighborhood though he didn't look it. Well, most of him didn't look it. Richie Lapking had very tough-looking eyes. He was also the best climber in the neighborhood.

Chicago is a typical midwestern town. Flat. A pitcher's mound is considered a decent-size hill. In this neighborhood, when a kid hit a certain age, he started climbing things. I don't know why. Buildings, light poles, trees.

Some kids were experts in one area. Timothy Snyder, for instance, was a brilliant light pole man. But the master of them all was Richie Lapking. His favorite were trees.

On windy days, he'd go to one of the tallest trees in the neighborhood and climb to within a few feet of the top. You'd look up there and see Richie Lapking riding the winds as they gusted through the branches. A bronco buster with an oak tree for a horse. He hardly seemed to be holding on at all.

I once asked Richie Lapking why he did that and he said because it was a great place to think about life. When I took philosophy in college, I found it difficult to imagine Plato getting his most creative thoughts at the end of a tree.

We're playing softball here one day. Richie Lapking is playing third base. I'm batting. I hit a ground ball that somehow squeezes between third base and Richie. For some reason, the left fielder is playing way off the line. It's obvious to everyone that with my speed I'm going to be able to leg out a home run. A rare moment indeed.

But making the turn around first base, I slip and fall. Now I'll be lucky if I get to second. Everyone begins smirking and laughing. The left fielder has reached the ball and is getting ready to throw it into the infield. Richie Lapking speaks. "Let him have it."

We are all stunned, no one more so than me. But I do have enough brains to savor the moment. I go into "the home run trot." As I come around third base, I tip my hat to the crowd even though there is no crowd and I'm wearing no hat. As I cross the plate, it is made clear to me that I've taken, perhaps, a bit too long. The next hitter is already standing at the plate and the pitch almost hits me in the head.

When there wasn't a game to get into, either on the street or at the park, Paul, Warren, and I would go to the park and "hit 'em out." One guy would toss up the ball and hit it and the other two would play the outfield. We'd do it for hours.

Drifting back for that long, high fly ball, pounding my fist into the glove, in front of thousands of fans, waiting for the last out of the big game. I loved it.

When autumn came and everybody else started playing football, Paul, Warren, and I would go to the park and "hit 'em out." We'd do that until there was snow on the ground. Catching a line drive in November was like using the palm of your hand to stop a two-ton dart.

When the snows finally did come, I'd get attacks of "baseballitis." In school, instead of studying, I'd draw diagrams of baseball diamonds. Or I'd casually walk through the living room and scoop up my little brother to start the double play.

When Brian was about the age I was then—

eleven years old—Melinda thought it would be a good idea if we sent him to an acting coach. I didn't. Finally, I agreed. There were a series of them. The good ones recognized his talent and realized that there was little they could add. The bad ones tried.

Walking back to the house and climbing up the three steps. Standing right in front of the door. I even take out the key. Debating whether or not to go in. Maybe I'll take a walk. I've waited twenty years, a few more minutes aren't going to make any difference.

The phone begins ringing again. I wait. It'll stop. But it doesn't. Opening the storm door. Sliding the key into the lock. Turning. Hearing the bolt slide back into the door. Pushing, very gently, the door eases open. A fragrance. Home.

6

The phone stops ringing. Looking around, I see that almost nothing has changed. Ma's reading lamp at the end of the couch. Both the couch and the matching chair are still covered in plastic. Remembering Dad's joke. "Nice to know that after the nuclear war there'll be a clean place to sit down."

Dad's easy chair.

The worn carpet where Danny used to sprawl when he watched television.

The television's new. My Christmas gift to Ma this year.

It is as if I have stepped into a three-dimensional memory. But memories are kinder; always out of focus and diluting reality until all that remains are subtle reminders of what once had been.

The reality of this moment is brutal. Part of me wants to believe they're all in the kitchen. Ma's making dinner, Dad's reading the newspaper, and Danny's helping set the table. Just as the pain is becoming too much, the ringing phone slaps my mind back to sobriety.

Ma just wanted to make sure she hadn't dialed wrong. Walking into the kitchen, dropping my spiral notebook on the counter as I pick up the phone.

"Hello."

"Donald, where have you been? I was getting worried. I've been calling and calling . . ."

"Hi, Ma. I heard the phone ringing before but I just couldn't find my key in time."

"You had trouble with the lock, didn't you? You've always had—"

"No, Ma. I just couldn't find the key."

"You didn't lose it again, did you?"

"No, Ma."

"How long has it been since you've been home? It can't be twenty years!"

"Twenty years, Ma."

"That's a long time to be away from home, Donald. I can't believe you've stayed away that long. Twenty years, I just can't believe you've stayed away from home that long, Donald."

"Yeah, Ma . . ."

"Now, don't you feel foolish waiting all that time?"

"No, Ma. Can I get off the phone now?"

"Where are you?"

"Where am I? Ma, there's only one phone in the house."

"I don't appreciate you talking smart to me."

"I'm not trying to be smart. I'm in the kitchen."

"Now, do you know where the garage is?"

"Of course, I know where the garage is. You haven't moved it, have you?"

"Donald."

"Sorry, Ma."

"That wasn't very funny."

"No, I didn't think it was funny either."

"Did you find the brown box in the guest closet?"

"I just walked in, Ma. I haven't had a chance."

"Since you left, I've been thinking . . . if it's not there, I'm almost certain that it's just inside the garage door. It would be on your left—"

"Okay, Ma, I'll check both places."

"It could even be in the basement."

"I'll look there, too."

"It might even be in the upstairs bedroom."

"Ma, I don't want to go up there."

"For heaven's sake, why not?"

"I just don't."

"Well, I can't see why—"

"I'll find the box. As soon as I do, I'll call you, okay?"

"Call me the moment you find it. You know how important that box is to—"

"Ma, I'll call you."

"What's your hurry?"

"Ah, I've got to go to the bathroom."

"Call me."

"I will."

"Love you."

"Love you, too, Ma."

Hanging up the phone. I spend a couple of seconds searching for my pack of cigarettes before I remember that I'm trying to quit . . . and why. Thinking about the two emergency cigarettes in my shirt pocket. Maybe I should just throw them away. I decide against it.

Seeing by the clock on the wall that it's not even

nine o'clock yet, I'll call the doctor's office around four. That'll be two o'clock in L.A. They've got to know by then.

As I look around the kitchen, I do notice a few new things: refrigerator, the microwave. There goes the inheritance.

The phone's different, too. But it's in the same place on the counter where the phone's always been. Used to call Donna Trandelli almost every night, but not for long. Not much privacy in the kitchen.

I think about how fascinating it would be if I could pick up that phone and dial old phone numbers and the person would still be there. Not just there but the way they were then.

Depressing. That kind of thinking's a sign of middle age dread.

Hungry. It's not even been twelve hours since I've quit smoking but I seem to be spending half my time looking for cigarettes I don't have and for food I can't have.

Opening the refrigerator and finding a bottle of diet pop, leaning against the counter as I drink it. Maybe this will fill me up. Noticing the space between the refrigerator and the basement door. That's where the dog's dish used to be kept.

We had gone over to Uncle Carl's. His dog had just had another litter, the fourth one in five years. My Aunt Helen called her "the slut of the South Side."

Every year, Danny and I had campaigned. Finally, Dad surrendered and said we could have a dog.

Danny wanted the runt while I wanted the biggest one. Uncle Carl encouraged my dad to take the runt because the other pups might be sold for a few bucks each.

Uncle Carl pointed to the runt and whispered

darkly. "If no one wants him, boys, well . . . you know what might happen." Capital punishment might not be much of a crime deterrent but just the slightest hint of it kept those doggies moving.

Danny and I decided to name the dog Blackie. He was an all-white dog. We thought that was very clever.

It bothered Ma that we didn't know anything about the dog's background. I don't know why. We didn't know that much about ours.

Looking around the kitchen. Remembering. Pulling out a drawer that used to be the junk drawer. Still is. Looks like the same junk.

Thinking about the beginning of Brian. The very beginning. He owes his existence to a junk drawer and a rain storm.

7

Early April. A time of the year when even the days aren't sure if it's winter or spring. Melinda and I are getting ready to leave the house. We are going to the formal opening of a play that evening. I'm wearing a tuxedo and—I can't remember exactly what Melinda is wearing but she looks more beautiful than I have ever seen her before.

Hearing the wind outside whip around the house as we grab for coats, the car keys finally in my hands. We are running very late and Melinda has decided it's my fault.

"I can't believe," she hisses, "that you would put both sets of keys in that junk drawer. We wasted at least twenty minutes looking all over the house for them before you remembered where they were. Then you waste another ten minutes going through that drawer looking for them."

"I told you, it was an accident. I wasn't thinking."

"You couldn't find a car, much less the keys, in that drawer," says Melinda. "I've asked you a million times to clean it out."

"I like it that way."

"We could have been there by now," she says. "I think you did it deliberately. If you didn't want to go to this play, you should have just said so."

"I said it twenty different times," I reply.

"You don't want to go to anything where there isn't a score involved."

Melinda opens the laundry-room door and steps into the garage. Following right behind her, I hit the button on the wall, which activates the overhead door. Melinda stops abruptly and spins around, causing me to almost walk into her.

"I forgot my credit cards," she says.

"I have mine."

"I should have my own."

"Melinda, we are going to the theater, not to Europe."

Within the few seconds that it has taken us to exchange those words, the overhead door has swung up and a storm has erupted directly over the house.

Rockets of rain are exploding on the driveway. Sparks of water, carried by the wind, are singeing the interior of the garage, spraying Melinda and me.

"Move it," I say. "I'm getting drenched." We both hurry and get into the car.

Melinda sits in her seat, shivering. "I'm cold. Turn on the heat."

"The car has to warm up first." It's an exchange we have had approximately eighty million times.

Backing the car out onto the driveway. The rain is coming down so hard that within a few feet of leaving the garage, we can no longer see it. After I hit the remote control button, there is no familiar whirl of the garage door coming back down. But it's not until I back the car down the driveway and park in front of the house that we can see that the garage door is still up. I aim the remote control at the garage and fire repeatedly. Nothing. "There's something wrong here."

"Really?" says Melinda mockingly.

I glare at her but her eyes refuse to accept the challenge.

"The storm's probably knocked out the electricity," she says.

"I've got to get the door down," I say. "With the wind blowing the way it is, everything in the garage is going to get soaked."

The car engine sputters, mumbles a few apologies, and dies. Turning the ignition and pumping the pedal. Nothing.

"Now what?" demands Melinda.

"Vapor lock," I say with authority.

"What is vapor lock?"

"How the hell should I know? That's what my father always said when a car wouldn't start in the rain."

"Maybe it's flooded," she says.

"No."

"How do you know?"

"Because my father never said that, at least in the rain."

"How can a man know so little about cars?" exclaims Melinda. "Last month, didn't you oversee the writing of the owners' manual for that Swedish car company?"

"Yes, at the same time you were writing that pamphlet on venereal disease for the AMA. Do you have any hands-on experience in that area?"

Melinda doesn't respond to my remark. She simply stares at the windshield as waves of rain continue to splatter against it. "Doesn't matter," she says blankly. "It's raining too hard right now to drive anyway. I've never seen it rain this hard this long."

"It's only been a few minutes," I say.

"But look at how hard it's raining."

She's right. I have never in my life seen rain with such intensity. Glancing at my watch. "We still have plenty of time. We'll just sit here and wait a few minutes. By then, the rain will have let up, the vapor lock will be unlocked or the flood will be unflooded or the planets will be properly aligned, and the car will start. If the electricity's still out, I can always pull the garage door down manually."

Melinda simply shivers in reply.

But ten minutes later and twenty minutes later and thirty minutes and forty minutes later the rain has not let up, the car has not started, and the electricity has not gone back on. Throughout the entire time, Melinda and I hardly speak.

"The street's beginning to flood," says Melinda. "If we don't get back into the house now, we may not be able to."

I look at my watch again. "We still have time to make the show."

"No," says Melinda flatly. "I've never seen this street hold water before. If it's this bad here, there has to be flooding all over the city."

"You know, Melinda, I have seen you carry an umbrella on the sunniest day, where there wasn't a cloud in the sky, just because you "felt" it might rain. But I didn't see one in your hands tonight."

Midway through my words, Melinda drops her head into her hand. "I forgot."

Putting my hand on the handle as I build up the courage to throw open the door. "One . . ." I begin counting, "two . . ."

"Three," shouts Melinda as she flings open her door, springs out of the car, and begins running for the open garage.

I reach across the car and pull her door shut. A second later, I, too, am out of the car and sprinting for the shelter of the garage.

It makes no difference. Within a few feet, I am drenched. By the time I get to the garage, my feet are squishing inside my shoes. Melinda is standing in the middle of the garage. The rain has tightened her hair around her head and her dress around her body. The wind is blowing so furiously that droplets of rain continue to fly by her. She looks delicious. Momentarily distracted by her wet appeal, I don't realize that she is pointing at the rope handle, which is hanging over her head.

"Grab the damn handle and pull the door down."

"Oh . . . yeah, sure." I run over, leap up, grab the handle, and ride down with it as the garage door rumbles back down into place.

We are now standing in total darkness. The wind continues to slam the rain into the door, creating thunder inside the garage.

Hearing Melinda whisper somewhere behind me. "Now I know how the three little pigs felt."

"Where are you?" I ask.

"Over here."

Reaching for her hand and finding it. Guiding her, or her guiding me, I'm not sure which, toward the laundry room door. Discovering it, opening it, and stepping in. I automatically flip the light switch but nothing happens. We are still standing in the dark.

"Take off your shoes."

But even as Melinda is saying it, I'm already hopping around on one foot trying to untie the soaked laces.

"Oh, good idea," I say cynically. "I would have never thought of it."

I can hear that Melinda is now hopping around on one foot, too. She bumps into me. I skip back a step, hit a laundry basket, and go sprawling into a corner.

"Are you all right?" Melinda says into the darkness. Her voice is smudged with suppressed laughter. She answers her own question. "Yes, you are." She begins laughing out loud.

"Do you realize," I say from my sitting position in the corner, "that you are basically laughing at a blind man?"

"No," Melinda corrects me. "I am laughing at a blind, stupid man. Big difference. I'm going into the family room," she says. "We can get some light from the gas fireplace."

After untangling myself from the laundry basket, I pull off my shoes and socks, and pad into the family room. The only light comes from the fireplace, which is already livid with flames. Melinda is staring into the fire as the wet dress clings to her body and the shadows of the flames flicker on her face. She looks over at me. "Well, we're staying home just like you wanted. Now are you satisfied?"

"No, but we can work on that."

The rain stamped its feet, the thunder roared its approval, and the lightning gave a standing ovation. Truly a great performance.

8

Still feeling hungry. It occurs to me that there are very few restaurants in this neighborhood. I guess if you want a good meal, you show up at home at five o'clock. There is a White Castle about six blocks from here. As I was saying, there aren't any restaurants in this neighborhood.

Actually, I love White Castle. When I was a kid, for a special treat, my dad would take the family there. What a place. Where else can you order eighty-five hamburgers at a time?

Over there, in that corner, there used to be a small wooden chair. When Danny and I were little kids, that's how Ma would punish us, by making us sit on The Chair for five minutes. But when you're a little kid, five minutes is a very, very long time.

One Sunday morning, I'm sitting on the chair. Dad's at the table, reading the newspaper. Ma walks by. He says to her, "I see where that cop killer is going to the chair."

Made sense to me.

That's something no one ever talks about. No one ever warns you. The clock, the one up here inside your head, how it starts out ticking so slowly.

First grade. It seems like I spent forty years there. Actually, it was only three.

Write it down. Taking the spiral notebook from the counter, flipping it open, and scribbling down the words *First grade/forty years.*

I remember coming home from my last day of first grade. A neighbor asked me how long I had off and I told her I had *"T-h-e s-u-m-m-e-r"* off. It was, like, forever. "I have eternity off." When you're six years old, you haven't even heard of September.

A few years later, I still had *"T-h-e s-u-m-m-e-r"* off, but now I'd heard about September. A few years after that, it was "Let's try and get together before the summer's over." Now, a blink of the eye.

"What was that?"

"Summer."

It's like a roller-coaster ride. That first hill, in terms of actual distance, isn't much of the ride at all. But it takes you forever to get up it. Click . . . click . . . click. Finally, you're at the top. Somewhere in your early twenties. What a view! Then, all of a sudden, you're shooting down that hill. *Whoosh!* In what seems like a moment, life tells you, "Get off." But you don't understand. "You see, I just got on and . . ."

"Get off."

I love it when people say they feel secure about themselves. Yeah, right. Here we are, living on this speck of dirt, going through space at eighty billion miles an hour. We don't know for certain where we came from or where we're going, but they feel secure. They're not secure. They're nuts.

Looking at the chairs around the table. Ma would sit there, in the chair closest to the stove, then Dad, Danny, and me.

Every night, Ma would give us two choices: take it or leave it.

Sometimes, Dad would dish out the food and he wasn't too neat about it. When I was a little kid, I was very finicky about such things. "Dad, the mash potatoes are touching the meat and the green peas are all over the place."

He'd say what every father has always said, "Ah, it's all going to the same place anyway." My dad. He would have made a great maître d'.

Ask him what was for dessert and he'd say, "Another piece of bread." Funny guy. Ma's favorite was Jell-O. I don't eat things that move that much.

I'm fifteen and Danny's twelve. One night, the family's sitting here eating dinner. We're all talking and grabbing for things. Dad says, "After supper, one of you boys better take out the garbage."

"You do it," I say to Danny. "I took it out this morning."

"But I took it out last night and there was a lot more then."

"You're going out to the garage anyway," I counter.

"No, I'm not."

"Liar. Just a few minutes ago, you said—"

"What I said was—"

Ma interrupts us. "You boys should treat each other better. Remember, your friends come and go, but you only have one brother."

Dad says, "I don't give a damn how you treat each other. One of you had better take out the garbage."

Danny and I play a game of scissors, paper, rock

to see who'll do it. A kid's game. You both make fists and shake them three times. On the third time, you do either two fingers, which is scissors; all five fingers, flat out, which is paper; or you just do your fist again, which is rock. Scissors cuts paper, paper covers rock, and rock breaks scissors. I realize it's not exactly chess, but it worked for us.

Danny won. He always did. I think he cheated.

A few minutes later, Danny and I are talking about something else. Dad has gotten off the garbage kick and is now telling us that our room looks like two slobs live there. How observant. Ma is standing by the sink. She looks back at us and that's when she says it, not to anyone in particular, almost to herself.

"Why can't it just stay this way? Why does it ever have to change?"

The rest of us get quiet. I don't know what she's talking about. Neither does Danny. Well, if he does, he doesn't say anything. Dad would never respond to something like that.

Then Danny knocks over his milk and Ma says, "See that's what you get for hurrying," and we're all back to talking and grabbing again.

The big dinner was on Sunday afternoon. In those days, you didn't have many choices. You got married. You had kids. Then, as the years passed, whether Ma liked it or not, things changed. Good-bye big dinners. Hello, McDonald's. Back then, people didn't have a "life-style." They had a life.

Quite often after Sunday dinner Dad would pile us all into the car and take us for a ride. We wouldn't go anywhere in particular. We'd just go for a ride. When I was a kid and I'd watch "Elliott Ness" on television, I remember thinking, My, they have a lot of Sunday dinners.

After every Thanksgiving dinner, Dad would say

the same thing. "You know, if the Russians had any brains, they'd attack us right now."

After the first year, no one would ask him why, but he'd tell us anyway. "It would be mighty tough defending ourselves while we're busy passing gas and wondering who's going to get to the leftovers first."

Sitting down at the table at "my place." This was also where Danny and I did our homework every night. Well, Danny did his homework. I have no idea what I was doing but it certainly wasn't my homework. Danny was a good student. Good athlete, too. But he had to work at his studies.

Me? You know how, in every class, there're four or five kids who never, ever do their homework? I was at least three of them.

I am fourteen and Danny's eleven. Lying in our beds waiting to fall asleep. "You know," says Danny, "history doesn't make any sense."

I'm exhausted and I really don't feel like talking. "Now what?"

"The President can be removed from office for 'high crimes and misdemeanors,' right?"

"So?"

" 'Misdemeanors?' What? He can be removed for littering?"

I roll over so my back's facing him. "Go to sleep."

"We also have to memorize the Gettysburg Address."

"Uh-huh."

Danny says, "You know that part where Lincoln says, 'The world will little note nor long remember . . .'?"

"Yeah?" I say.

"Hardly."

"Good point."

Sleep.

Every school day, before every subject, the teacher would say, "All right, whoever did not do their homework, stand." As I did so, nervously shuffling from foot to foot, I had to lie. What was I going to do? Tell the truth? "I didn't feel like doing my homework." Sure. By the time I was out of grammar school, my aunt had died fourteen different times.

It never occurred to me that it would have been a lot easier simply to do the homework. It just never occurred to me, for twelve years.

Sometimes, I'd really have to reach. "Well, ma'am, you see, I was sitting at the kitchen table doing my homework when all of a sudden a plane hit the back of the house. Fortunately, nobody got killed. That's why you won't read about it in the newspapers. But on the way out of the kitchen, one of the survivors stole my spelling homework. I have no idea why."

As a kid, you quickly figure out that the truth only works as an off-speed pitch. Use it every now and then and it'll catch them by surprise. That's the way it was with Ma. But, like most important lessons in life, I had to learn it the hard way.

One day Ma says to me, "Did you break the basement window?"

She has caught me off guard. I panic. I tell the truth. "Yeah, Ma, it was me."

Now it's her turn to be caught off guard. "Oh . . . I see . . . Well . . . that does change things. Since you told the truth . . . since you were honest . . . there will be no punishment."

What a deal.

Two days later, Ma asks me, "Are you the one who left grease on the guest towels in the bathroom?"

Smiling. "Yeah, Ma, I'm the guy." Ma proceeds to destroy me.

There's an old saying—I think Ma started it—"The truth hurts."

Oddly enough, Brian's always been honest with me. He prides himself on his integrity. Always tells the truth. As far as I know. Of course, he wants to be an actor where the whole idea is pretending to tell the truth.

I'm seventeen and Danny's fourteen. One night, we're sitting at the kitchen table doing our homework. Well, he's doing his.

I'm not much of an athlete, but I try. Even though Danny is three years younger, at that point he's as tall as I am, and he weighs more.

The next week, he is trying out for the freshman football team. I don't think he cares one way or the other about it, but I had encouraged him and I think that's why he's doing it.

"Danny," I say, "no matter what position you end up playing, you've got to know how to block to play football."

"I know that."

"I'm not much of a blocker, but I bet even I could knock you down."

Danny says, "I can't talk about it now. I've got to study."

"Using no hands . . ."

"Give me a break," Danny groans. "I've got a big biology test tomorrow."

"Come on," I challenge him, "Let's go outside. No hands, I bet I can knock you down."

He thinks about it a moment. "All right, but just for fifteen minutes. Then you leave me alone. I've got to study."

We go out on the front lawn. It's a cool fall night. We both fold our arms. I run at him and really give him a pop. Danny goes staggering back ten or fifteen feet. I go charging after him. But by the time I give him a second shot, he's already regained his balance. At least three different times, I get him wobbling, but I can't knock him down.

Two hours, we're out there. Finally, we look at each other. Silent agreement. Enough's enough. We start walking back toward the house. I put my hand on his shoulder.

"You're tougher than I thought."

"Yeah, well, I better be able to knock my biology teacher on his ass tomorrow or he's going to flunk mine."

As usual, that night, Danny is having trouble falling asleep. I'm exhausted. He starts talking about something and I interrupt him.

"Will you shut up? I've got to get some sleep."

Danny says, "You know, sleep's a funny thing. You can only enjoy it when you're awake and then you're not asleep . . . and if you have to get up, then it's real nice just lying here curled up under the blankets for a few extra minutes. But if you don't have to get up, then it's just lying around and that's boring. Interesting thought, isn't it?"

I say, "Danny, here's an interesting thought. Shut up or I'll kill you."

He doesn't. "I wonder if there's an afterlife. I mean, I wonder what's after this?"

"If you don't shut up, you're going to find out right now."

"No, really, what I mean . . ."

Putting my pillow over my head. If I had the strength, I'd put it over his head instead.

The next morning, when I wake up, I feel like someone has glued my arms to the bed. Then I realize they're so sore I can't move them. Discovering the challenge of getting dressed using only my teeth.

I presume Danny's in the same shape I'm in. But when I get downstairs to the kitchen, Danny is eating breakfast and seems to be having no problems at all.

Sitting down at the table, I feel like Charlie Mc-Carthy. If I really try, I can get my hands as high as the edge of the table. Skipping cereal since I don't feel like lapping it up like a dog.

Danny gets cut during the first week of freshman football tryouts. It doesn't seem to bother him at all.

That autumn, every Thursday afternoon, a group of us seniors would go to a park near the school and play touch football for a couple of hours. We would simply choose up sides and play.

Touch football is the only sport in which I've ever excelled. Since I could catch and run well, I was a great receiver.

The first few minutes of the afternoon would always be eaten up by everyone arguing to play quarterback. Since it was well known that I could throw a football, on my very best day, perhaps five yards, I was not included in these discussions.

The Thursday afternoon after Danny gets cut, we seniors are at the park getting ready to play touch football when we realize that we have an uneven number of guys. Just then, I see Danny walking by with a couple of girls.

''My brother's right over there,'' I volunteer.

One of the guys looks over, sees that Danny's

even bigger than I am, and says, "Sure, ask him if he wants to play."

Trotting over to Danny. This is a great chance for me to show him what a star I can be.

"How you doing, Donald?" he says. "Meet my two friends, Darlene and Veronica."

"Nice to meet you, girls," I say as I look past them. "Danny, how about some football? We need another guy."

"I don't think so," he says as he glances at the two girls. "We were going to get something to eat. Besides, I've had enough of football."

"Come on," I say. "One more guy and we'll have even sides."

The strain in my voice betrays how important this is to me. By the surprised expression on Danny's face, I can tell that he's detected it.

Danny looks at the girls. "Can we make it another time?"

Danny's on my team. For the first few series of downs, our team goes nowhere. Our quarterback, a guy named Ronald Felkoso, has a decent arm but he is telegraphing where he's going to throw the ball. He's already been intercepted twice.

Standing in the huddle. Felkoso says to Danny, "You stand in the quarterback position. That'll confuse them. I'll be over on the right side. When the ball's snapped to you, I'll take a step back behind the line of scrimmage. You flip the ball to me and run straight downfield deep."

Felkoso points to me and another guy. "You two flair to the left. Garger, you run down the right sideline. I'll look for the open man."

We break the huddle and get into formation. But as the ball is snapped to Danny, the guy covering Felkoso immediately reads the play and, as Felkoso steps behind the line of scrimmage, so does his defender. Danny can't throw over there. With two men in the backfield, it's now immediate rush.

Three guys come racing across the line after Danny. I yell at him to get his attention and then start running downfield with two guys covering me. As Danny runs to his left, he leaps into the air and launches the ball downfield. Fifty yards away, running full speed, I stretch out for the ball and catch it on the tips of my fingers for a touchdown. A perfect pass.

For the next hour, Danny throws long passes, short passes, and everything in between. When he has to, he drills it. When he has to, he floats the ball over the arms of outstretched defenders.

On one play, there are three guys covering me, yet Danny manages to throw the ball past all of them right into my arms. Our team scores every time we have the ball.

In the huddle, one of the guys complains to Danny. "You're throwing everything to your brother. I'm just as good a receiver as he is."

Danny looks at him and says, "He's my brother. You have to be better."

Walking home with Danny after the game. He is tossing the football up in the air.

"How could they have cut you from the freshman football team?" I ask. "Weren't you hustling during the tryouts?"

"Yeah, I guess so," says Danny.

"Boy, that's an aggressive answer."

"I don't know. You have to be there at certain times. You have to do what they tell you. I just don't like being on an organized team."

We are now walking down our street, about six houses away from our own.

"Maybe you haven't got the arm to play high school football," I chide him. "The guys you played with today aren't exactly great ball players."

"You're probably right," says Danny. He holds up the football. "Where do you want it?"

"Put it in the garage."

Danny reaches back and throws the ball. It easily clears the house we are approaching and disappears in the general direction of our garage.

Not even acknowledging the incredible throw, looking straight ahead as I speak to Danny. "Obviously, your accuracy stinks. I said in the garage, not over it."

Walking into the living room. Making it a point not to look around. Opening the guest closet. Mostly empty hangers. Ma's winter coat. A pair of boots. An umbrella hanging from a hook. An open but empty shoe box sits on the otherwise barren shelf. There is no brown box.

It's the first time I've ever seen the closet so empty. In its prime, I often couldn't even find a place to hang my jacket. I'd end up throwing it up on the shelf or dropping it on the floor.

With the first cold day, I'd pull on my heavy coat. As I stuck my hands into the pockets, if I was lucky, I would discover treasures that I had forgotten about since last winter; perhaps a package of M&Ms or some loose change. But never a ticket to Hawaii.

Looking at my watch. Still have plenty of time to find the brown box. Not quite ready to go through the rest of the house. At least I've gotten the big toe wet. Time to take a break.

I decide to take a walk through the neighborhood. See how it's changed. See how I have.

Reaching for the front door, I notice, once again,

Ma's new color television. Naturally, she's put it right where the television "always goes."

I'm thirteen and Danny's ten. The television has just returned from a three-week stay in the repair shop. I am watching my favorite television show "Mr. Ed" and laughing hysterically. Danny walks in, looks at the show for a moment, and then says to me:

"You know, he's not really talking."

"What?"

"The horse. He's not really talking. It's a voice-over. You know that."

Very annoyed. "Yeah, I know that. What's your point?"

"No point," Danny says. "It just seems like you were forgetting that." Danny walks out the front door.

Now I'm not laughing anymore. Yelling after him, "Thanks for reminding me."

Suddenly, I realize what Danny's just done. I remember what his favorite show is and run out onto the front porch. Danny's walking down the street. Yelling at him, "Hey, Danny, hey . . . did you know Lassie's a boy?"

I don't even notice that Dad's sitting on the front step reading the newspaper. He looks up at me, truly puzzled.

"You mean there's a guy inside that dog?"

9

With my spiral notebook tucked under my arm, I walk out of the house, down the steps, and back onto the sidewalk again. You can drive the streets a million times, but the only way you can really feel a neighborhood is to walk it.

A squirrel scampers across a lawn. Ma hates them. Says they're just rats who know how to dress.

As I walk, I realize that I am retracing the three-block trip to Gerald Fenning Elementary School.

I am eight and Danny is five. When he starts kindergarten, he insists to Ma that he doesn't need anyone to take him. He can find his own way to school. Without telling Danny, Ma makes me follow him.

During the first week, his teacher warns the class that they should report any suspicious characters to her. She has to define all three words for them. Danny turns me in.

When Danny was a child, he used to cry on Saturday and Sunday because he couldn't go to school. I used to cry the other five days of the week.

Standing in the playground, looking up at the windows of my eighth-grade classroom. Some kid is staring down at me. Suddenly, his head jerks toward the front of the classroom. Spotted.

The window looks the same. Mrs. Kramer was my teacher. Like all the great ones, every now and then she'd interrupt her teaching just to talk to us about what she thought was important in life.

One afternoon toward the end of the school year, right in the middle of math class, Mrs. Kramer put down her book, told us to do likewise, and began to talk about her feelings as a teacher.

"Children, when I was in fourth grade, even younger than you, I decided I wanted to be a teacher. I have never regretted that decision. I love what I do. But, sometimes, when I'm driving to school or driving home, I think about how important you are to me . . . and how important I am to you.

"Your parents, of course, are the most important teachers you will ever have in your life. But, for this year at least, I'm important, too.

"I try to make learning fun. I know I'm not always successful. In some way, perhaps a big way, but more likely than not a small way, I am affecting the kind of person you are and will become. I hope that effect is a good one.

"If, in these past eight months, I've said or done anything to hurt your feelings, I want you to know I am truly sorry and that it was certainly unintentional.

"During the year, many of you have said to me many times that you were doing your best. To be honest, I've often had trouble believing you. Now I'm saying it to you and please believe me. I'm doing my best. Now, what page were we on?"

The smartest kid in that class was Mary Kaukuka, who's now a teacher in one of Chicago's suburbs. The dumbest kid was Terrence Basington, who is now the school superintendent of that suburb.

Mark Kefurth was sitting in front of me. Samuel Orr was sitting behind me. Today, Kefurth is one of the biggest real estate developers in southern California. He's a millionaire many times over. I read his name in the newspapers all the time.

About five years after that day that Mrs. Kramer talked to us, Samuel Orr, driving through Idaho, robbed a restaurant and executed the forty-year-old cashier, a mother of four. He is serving a life sentence with no chance of parole. He has been in prison for the past twenty-six years. Another two lifetimes since listening to Mrs. Kramer.

It's hard to know who makes a difference and what kind of difference they make, but I still remember Mrs. Kramer telling us she wanted to.

For me, the best time of the entire week was Friday afternoon; just sitting there dreaming about two whole days off from school. Friday afternoon was even better than the weekend. Saturday and Sunday are reality. But Friday afternoon is pure hope and that's always better.

The problem with school was that once the teacher decided you were a jerk, that was it. You'd never change her mind. You were always a jerk.

In fourth grade, the teacher puts this math problem on the board and no one can get the right answer. She's calling on all the heavy hitters, in other words, all the girls. Nothing. She's getting so desperate that she's even beginning to call on some of the boys.

Now sometimes when a teacher presents a problem to the class and they can't get the answer, it suddenly becomes more than just a problem. It becomes that teacher's entire career. Their professional reputation is on the line. With this one, you could just see the frustration ballooning up in her face.

Of course, all the time I'm jumping up and down in my desk, waving both hands. Every now and then, she looks over, gives me a pathetic sneer, and calls on somebody else.

After she calls on everybody else, she looks over at me and, in a tone of forced patience, says, "Well, Mr. Cooper, what do you think's the correct answer?"

"Mister." Whenever a teacher doesn't like you, it's always "mister," even if you're a girl.

I calmly stand up and state, "The correct answer is seventeen."

She's astounded. She says, "That's right! The correct answer is seventeen." But she's hardly about to compliment me. She says to the class, "Well, if even Mr. Cooper can get the right answer, if even this guy knows what's going on, what is wrong with the rest of you?"

She goes on that way for at least five minutes. But somewhere during that monologue, she and I become friends. Finally, she looks over and says, "Donald . . ." It's "Donald" now. "Donald, would you mind explaining to the rest of the class how even you managed to get the right answer?"

I say, "Not at all." Proudly, I stand up, walk to the blackboard, point to that problem, and say, "I guessed."

She never spoke to me again.

* * *

Walking toward 111th Street, which has a strip of commercial stores that trim the ends of the residential streets.

Wondering about the results of the biopsy. Looking at my watch. In less than six hours, I'll know.

Since I found out, two weeks ago, about the shadow on my lung, I catch myself constantly monitoring me to see if I am getting out of breath. As I walk now, I'm even tempted to take my own pulse, but in this neighborhood you don't hold your own wrist.

When I reach my corner, I see that the little grocery store is no longer there. It's been replaced by a tanning salon. A sign of the times. I don't know anyone in southern California who goes and sits in a freezer twice a week.

When I was growing up, the national anthem of our family, sung daily by Ma and Dad and danced to by Danny and me, was "Will one of you boys run to the store and . . ."

One hundred eleventh Street was the "busy" street in the neighborhood. You had to live at least double-digit years before you were allowed to cross it. As a kid, even though you might live only half a block from another kid who lived on the other side of 111th Street, you might as well have been in another galaxy.

In fifth grade, when we read about the courage of the great explorer, Christopher Columbus, I decide to go for it. That afternoon after school, I head for 111th Street.

In this neighborhood, when you're a child, you discover that all adults share the same brain. When I am waiting to cross 111th Street, two adults ask me where I think I'm going. During the twenty minutes

I am on the other side of 111th Street, another two adults ask me what I am doing over there. As soon as I get back, another adult tells me I had no business crossing 111th Street. The moment I walk in the house, Ma shouts at me, "Mister, you're in very big trouble. . . ."

All the neighborhood parades are held up here on 111th Street.

I am nine and Danny is six. Sometimes he can be a very strange kid. One day I bring him up here for a parade. So, the parade's over, the crowd's breaking up, and we're heading home. Danny starts crying. I say, "What's wrong with you? Didn't you like the parade?"

"Yeah."

"Then what are you crying about?"

"I don't know . . . the end."

"The end?"

Danny says, "Yeah, the end. I really loved the parade. I was having such a great time. Then, all of a sudden, there it was, the end. I just felt like crying."

Danny was a crier. He'd go to a movie and if he felt like it he'd cry. He'd be reading a book and he'd be crying. He'd even cry when he watched the news on television. Well, he wouldn't actually cry during the news. He'd think about something for a while and then start crying during prime time.

I used to mock him for it but it didn't do any good. Danny was like that until he was at least nine or ten. Then he became the world's greatest pouter.

I'm fourteen and Danny's eleven. A cool, cloudy summer Saturday afternoon. I am getting dressed to go to a neighborhood carnival. At the park the day before I'd met some girl and asked her to go with me. Danny walks into the bedroom.

"Ma said you're going to the carnival?"

"Yeah, so?"

"You promised you'd take me."

"When did I say that?"

"Last Sunday," says Danny. "Right after dinner. I asked you and you promised."

"Are you sure?"

"Ma was there," says Danny. "She remembers 'cause I just asked her."

I finish buttoning my shirt. "No problem," I say. "The carnival doesn't close until tomorrow. We'll go then."

"We can't go tomorrow," says Danny. "Dad's company picnic is tomorrow."

Ma walks into the room. Not a good sign.

"Look, Danny, I can't take you today. I've already made other plans."

"You promised me first."

"Maybe it'll rain tomorrow and they'll have to cancel the picnic. Then we can go to the carnival."

"If it rains," says Danny, "they'll close the carnival, too."

"Who are you going with?" Ma asks.

"Probably some girl," Danny says.

"A friend," I reply.

"You haven't got any friends," says Danny. "It's a girl and it's got to be a first date. Nobody would go out with you twice."

"I'm not going to make you take Danny—" Ma begins.

"The heck with him," Danny interrupts. "He doesn't have to take me if he doesn't want to." He plops down on the bed, folds his arms behind his head, and pouts up at the ceiling.

"I'm not going to make you take Danny," Ma repeats. "But as I've told you before, your friends come and go but you only have one brother."

Sliding my wallet into my back pocket, grabbing my keys, and ignoring Ma's comment as I walk out the door. I say, "Danny's probably got a million things to do today."

Danny shouts to make sure I hear it as I leave the room. "I've got nothing to do today. Nothing."

I have a miserable time. It starts raining as soon as this girl, I can't remember her name, as soon as she and I get there so all the rides close down.

Then she runs into an old boyfriend and proceeds to talk to him for at least an hour. All the time, I'm just hanging around like a jerk waiting for her to shut up.

Finally, she turns to me and says, "Bobby's offered to give me a ride home."

His name I remember.

"He lives right near me and since it's raining, I'm sure you don't mind."

The moment I leave the protection of the carnival tents, it begins pouring so I'm drenched by the time I get home.

Walking into the bedroom, Danny is still lying on his bed. "Haven't you moved since I left?" I ask.

Danny wouldn't even look at me. "I told you I didn't have anything to do."

I can't even remember her name.

Walking by a coffee shop where a bakery used to be. A small man is sitting at the counter, reading a newspaper, drinking a cup of coffee. His shoulders are so broad that it appears as if his head is sitting in the middle of a shelf. His arms seem to be made of coiled steel. He is wearing a black T-shirt, jeans, and steel-tip shoes. The face is familiar. Aged, but familiar.

What initially disorients me is that he is almost the same height as when I last saw him, which is over thirty years ago. He is the man who, literally, loves life on a limb, Richie Lapking.

A tinkling bell on the door announces my entrance. I sit down next to him and wait a moment until his eyes leave the newspaper.

"Richie, remember me?"

One of his hands reaches for his cup of coffee while the other grabs my shoulder. "Cooper, so what have you been up to?" As if he had seen me yesterday.

The waitress walks over, I don't recognize her, and I order a cup of coffee. "I moved out of the neighborhood, you know. . . ."

"Oh, yeah, I remember somebody telling me that."

"Twenty years ago . . ."

"I guess that's why I haven't seen you around lately." Richie turns his attention back to the newspaper for a moment. "Those White Sox lost another one by a run."

"How are they doing?" I realize my mistake the instant I say it, but it's too late.

Richie Lapking looks at me, puzzled. "You don't know?"

"Well, I've kind of been following the Cubs lately." I might as well have told him I had a sex change operation.

Chicago is not one city. It is two: the North Side and the South Side. The Cubs and their fans are on the North Side while the White Sox and their worshipers are on the other side of town.

There are a few fans living on the wrong side of the city. I can think of two kids I grew up with who were Cubs fans. There's even a rumor that a Yankee fan survives somewhere in the city. But, generally, Chicago baseball fans live among their own.

An old joke. Ask a White Sox fan who his favorite team is and he'll say, "The White Sox and whoever's playing the Cubs."

I open the spiral notebook and write it down. Maybe, in L.A., it'll be a new joke.

Richie Lapking has gone back to looking at his newspaper.

"I live in L.A. now," I try to explain. "I get the Cubs on cable out there. I never get a chance to watch the Sox."

"Yeah, sure."

I take a sip of my coffee while looking straight ahead. "So what's Ronnie doing?" Ronnie's his younger brother.

Richie looks back at me. "He's an accountant. Has his own company now."

"Pretty smart kid, huh," I comment.

Richie says, "Did you know I was on the honor roll in high school all four years?"

"No."

"Yeah. All four years. I mean, Ronnie's not stupid, but he wasn't on no damn honor roll for four years either. But that kind of work," says Richie, "is too damn boring.

"You know," he says, "I can say this because he's my brother, Ronnie's the cheapest bastard in the world. I think that's why he went into accounting. He just loves to keep track of money even if it isn't his. The guy's a cheap bastard, I tell you."

"I wouldn't know."

"Even if you did," says Richie, "you wouldn't say it because he's my brother."

On the South Side of Chicago, comments and threats are often contained within the same words.

"You'll love this," says Richie. "He lives up near Wrigley Field now. In fact, he owns that three-story apartment building across the street from Wrigley Field. The one that's straight down the right field foul line."

Wrigley Field, home of the Cubs, is the only major league park in the world that is surrounded by residential buildings. People who own them can go up on their roofs and look right into the ballpark. Often, they're closer to home plate than fans in the cheap seats of other major league parks.

"Yeah, I know the building you're talking about," I say. "I see it on television all the time. That must be great."

"The previous owner," says Richie, "put outdoor carpeting up there, a wet bar—even a toilet."

I ask, "How do you and Ronnie like watching the games up there?"

Richie Lapking looks directly at me. "How would we know? We're Sox fans."

Time to make a peace offering. "Want a donut?"

"Nah."

I ask the waitress for a chocolate one for myself. "So what are you doing now, Richie?"

"Iron worker, Local Four thirty-eight. Been working on the Princeton Building on Wacker Drive for the past four months. Night shift."

"Do you," I asked, "work pretty high up, I mean, without much around you?"

"For the past ten days, I've been on the forty-seventh floor. Sometimes we walk on floors that are fairly completed. But we do a lot of skeletal work, too."

"How do you ever get used to that?" I ask, but Richie talks through my comment.

"Last night," he says as he stares out the window, "it was so clear, you could see all the way across the lake to Michigan. Goddamn, it was gorgeous." His mind savors the memory for a moment before he turns his attention back to me. "You know, I was straining so hard to see across the lake, I almost fell off the goddamn beam."

Richie Lapking chuckles to himself so I join in. "So what have you been up to, Cooper?"

"I'm a comedy writer." If I had told him I was a sheepherder, he couldn't have been more impressed.

Richie smiles at me weakly. "You can make a living doing something like that?"

"Yeah?" I answer with a question in my voice as if I'm not so sure either. I name some of the television shows I've written for. Richie has never watched any of them. I mention the major comedians I've worked with. Richie has heard of only two of them and thinks neither one is funny. Then he recalls that one of the other comedians I've mentioned had been on television just a few nights ago.

"You know what he says, Donny . . ."

I have forgotten that the kids in the neighborhood called me Donny. I have forgotten deliberately.

"This guy says, 'I'm from New York and we have a lot to be proud of.' Let's see . . ." says Richie as he tries to remember the rest of the joke. "Oh yeah, he says, 'Just last week, there was an article in *Time* magazine that said that the nation's largest producer of vegetables is now the New York Public School System.' "

Richie laughs even though he has told the joke. "Did you write that one?"

"Yeah," I say humbly. I didn't.

"Funny stuff. That's very funny stuff." Richie slaps me on the shoulder as he holds up his cup to signal to the waitress that he wants more coffee. My stock has just risen considerably.

"Betty," Richie says to the waitress as he refills his cup, "I'd like to you meet Donny Cooper. Used to live around here. He's a comedy writer now. You know, television. Stuff like that."

Betty gives the obligatory smile. "Nice to see you, Donny. How about a refill?"

"No, thanks."

Betty moves on to the other customers with her pot.

"You know," says Richie, "there's some guys I work with, two in particular, they're funnier than anybody I've seen on TV."

"Well," I say, "there is a big difference between being funny with people you know and making strangers laugh."

"Yeah," says Richie, "I'm sure you're right. The great ones make it look easy, right, Donny?"

"That's right."

"You'd be amazed," he said, "how many people think they can be iron workers."

I change my mind and ask Betty for that second cup of coffee and then order two more chocolate donuts. God, am I hungry. Coffee and donuts. I can't stand it any longer. But I still don't want to use one of my two emergency ones. "Richie, you got a cigarette?"

"Nah, I quit about eight years ago. Disgusting habit. I'm surprised a guy like you smokes."

"Not really . . . every now and then, I like to have one. . . . I've cut back quite a bit."

"Very bad for you."

"I know." How low have I sunk? I'm now getting health hints from a man who spent his childhood at the top of trees and his adult years hundreds of feet in the air where he almost falls off a beam trying to see two states away.

"So how did you become a comedy writer?"

I give him the short version. "I don't know, Richie. I started writing for one comedian and then he told some of his friends about me. . . . You know . . ."

"Networking," says Richie.

"Yeah, that's it, networking."

Says Richie, "Isn't that just another word for making friends you can use?"

"Pretty much."

Realizing to myself that the short version answer to Richie's question isn't much shorter than the long version.

After the divorce, I have no reason to stay at my job writing instruction manuals. But, then again, I have nowhere to go. One night after work I stop in at a comedy showcase. Fifteen comedians perform. At their best, most of them are forgettable, at their worst, embarrassing. But three of them have a strong stage presence, a nice rhythm to their work, great ideas. But they can't write.

After each one comes offstage, I talk to him, tell him how I can help. Within a year, I am writing for the best of the rising young comedians and for the mediocre of the older, falling ones.

The money isn't nearly as much as I am making on my day job but I quit the day job anyway. Move from a two-bedroom apartment in a nice neighborhood to a studio apartment above a Thai restaurant. I figure I can only be in one room at a time anyway. People just thought I had changed colognes.

Time to change the subject. "So where are you living now, Richie?"

"Same place."

"The same house you grew up in?"

"Yeah. The old man died about fourteen years

ago. I fixed up the basement into a real nice apartment for Ma. She just had her eightieth birthday."

"Is she still sharp?"

"Ma was never what you'd call sharp."

"Let me put it another way, Richie. Is she as sharp as she ever was?"

"No. But she's funnier than she ever was. I married Pat Moskatto, you know . . ."

"That blonde who lived on the corner of A hundred and fifth and Spaulding?" I ask.

"That's her."

"A gorgeous girl."

"Still is," says Richie. "We have three kids: a daughter who's in high school, one in junior college, and my son, the oldest, he's an apprentice iron worker with me. How about you?"

"One son, just graduated from college. I'm divorced. Have been for many years."

Richie laughs. "You Hollywood guys are all alike." His voice turns somber and his head nods affirmatively. "Just kidding, you know, Donny. Plenty of that stuff around here too, you know."

"Yeah," I nod right along with him.

"Hey, you know what the major cause of divorce is?" asks Richie impishly.

I've heard the joke a million times but I feign ignorance.

"No, what?"

"Marriage."

"Very funny."

"You can use it if you want," says Richie.

"Thanks. You know, Richie, when you were a kid, floating around up there in the tops of those trees, just watching you frightened me."

He takes a sip of his coffee. "I was scared to death."

"What?" I am stunned.

"Every time I did it. Scared to death. You know what I used to think about when I was up there? How the hell I was going to get down. Scared shitless."

"When did you get used to it?"

"Never did."

"But now you're working on those high buildings . . ."

"That scares the hell out of me, too. Every time."

"Then why do you do it?" I ask.

"To be honest I don't know," says Richie. He thinks about it a moment. "I don't know . . . I guess it's just the pure excitement of it, you know what I mean?" He looks at me and decides. "No, you don't."

Richie drains his cup of coffee. "Remember Oswego?"

"Yeah?"

"He's a doctor now. And Stibeck? He owns a huge plastics factory in Florida."

"You know, Richie," I say, "you're one of the smartest guys around here. Maybe the smartest."

Richie Lapking smiles. "This is true."

"You could have been anything you wanted to be."

Richie looks at me. He is truly puzzled by my statement. "But I am."

He drains his coffee cup and then continues with his cavalcade of neighborhood characters. "And Bobby Polhurst, he was doing real well in advertising until he dove into the wrong end of a neighbor's pool. Broke his neck."

"What a shame," I say, "he was such a great athlete."

"You know," says Richie, "he can still touch the rim on a backboard."

"Richie," I say, "let's be honest here. Bobby's

over six feet tall. A lot of men, even in their forties, who are that tall can still touch the rim."

"Donny, the man's in a goddamn wheelchair."

For an instant, I buy it. Then we both start laughing.

"You know, Donny," says Richie, "I think I could do your job."

"Yeah, I'm sure you could, Richie."

I decide it's time to thank him for one of the high moments of my youth, my one and only "home run trot."

"Say, Richie, remember when we were kids . . . we were all playing softball on the street one day and I hit this ball that looked like it was going to roll forever. A sure home run. I didn't get too many of those, you know. But I fell and then you said—"

"No."

" 'No' what?" I asked.

"No, I don't remember," says Richie as he gets up to leave.

"Oh," I reply. I can't tell if he's lying or not, but I'm not about to challenge him. He's not the kind of guy you want to ruffle the wrong way. Richie may enjoy being scared shitless but I don't.

Richie leaves his tip on the counter, waves goodbye to the waitress, and heads for the door. Looking back over his shoulder, he says, "It was great talking to you, Donny. See you around."

Betty, the waitress, watches him leave. "He's a regular guy, you know." Her way of saying that he is anything but.

A few minutes later, I'm standing on a corner where a motorist has just been pulled over by the police for going through a yellow light. The officer is young, trim, and very official. He is saying to the driver, "Sir, do you know why I pulled you over?"

They always say that. Three years ago, when I got pulled over for speeding in L.A., that's exactly what the cop said. It had crossed my mind but I didn't have the guts to say it. "Gee, Officer, I sure hope it doesn't have anything to do with those two bodies in the trunk."

Maybe I can use that. Flipping open the spiral notebook and stopping for a moment to write. As I do so, I can hear that this guy has no more courage than I do.

"Well, Officer, I'm in kind of a rush, and the light just turned yellow when I drove through it . . ."

How do yellow lights know when you're in a hurry?

A block later I turn a corner, and when I look at where it should be, I see instead a small complex of apartments standing where the Little League field once was.

Paul Godding and I are on the same Little League team. With the exception of Paul, it is a hideous group. I actually play first string. We have a game scheduled for two o'clock on a Sunday afternoon. On the previous Monday, it begins raining and it doesn't stop until Sunday at one o'clock.

The sky remains dark and threatening but I put on my uniform and walk over to Paul Godding's house. He is already walking down his steps in his uniform. When we get to the park, we see that the entire field is under water. Even the pitcher's mound.

A car pulls into the parking lot. A guy gets out, wearing hip boots and a raincoat, and walks over to us. It's our manager. He says to us, through gritted teeth, "Gentlemen, I left my easy chair, got my boots out of the basement, which is flooded, went to the garage, which is also flooded, and drove all the way over here just to tell you . . . there is no game.''

This is also the field where Danny played his first, and last, organized baseball game.

I am twelve and Danny is nine. From the time I am eight years old, I try out for the Little League every year. But I don't make it until I am eleven. Danny tries out when he's nine, makes it, and, before the season starts, is told by his manager that he will be one of the few nine-year olds in the league to play first string.

Ma and I go to his first game. Dad's working late that night. Even though Danny's only nine, anyone who cares to notice can see that he has the potential to be a great athlete. He has a strong throwing arm and is an exceptionally fast runner. Danny can catch anything that's hit near him. He is quick, well coordinated, and has that quiet confidence the great ones usually have. There is one small problem. Danny doesn't care.

In the fifth inning, a ground ball hit to him takes a strange bounce and pops him in the face, just above his right eye. Half of Danny's forehead swells up.

Ma and I take him over to the emergency room and have a doctor look at him just to make sure there are no internal injuries. The doctor says that by to-morrow Danny will have a big black-and-blue mark along with the swelling but that within another couple of days both the discoloring and the swelling will be gone.

Driving home. I am sitting in the backseat feeling rather proud of Danny. The first rule in fielding a ground ball is to stay in front of it and Danny has obviously accomplished that. Besides, getting wounded in the line of duty is always a little glamorous even if that duty is only playing shortstop in the Little League.

Ma keeps asking Danny if he's sure he's feeling all right.

"Hey, Danny," I say, "don't worry. Your next game isn't until Tuesday and you'll be able to play by then."

"I'm not worried," says Danny matter-of-factly, "because I'm quitting."

"What?" I scream it.

"I'm quitting."

Ma says, "Well, Danny, if I were you I wouldn't make that decision tonight. But you certainly don't have to play baseball if you don't want to."

I am going berserk in the backseat. "Why?"

Danny says, "Because I don't like getting hit in the head with hard objects. Who needs it?"

I bellow at him, "You candy-ass—"

Ma bellows back. "You do not use that kind of language."

"You wimp, you coward, you chicken . . . You're . . . you're nothing but a quitter."

Danny speaks slowly but emphatically. "That's what I'm telling you."

Leaving 111th Street and walking back along the residential streets. Two blocks and a turned corner later, I am once again standing in front of the house.

Usually, my dad would park his potato chip truck in the alley. But every now and then he'd put it right out here, in front of the house. I loved that. It was the biggest truck you ever saw. The other kids were impressed.

If I was feeling unusually generous, I'd take a few chosen ones through the truck for a brief tour. The fragrance of potato chips was everywhere. It never occurred to me until years later that walking through that truck always made me thirsty.

Sitting down on the top step. When I was a little kid, and I had a day off from school, sometimes my dad would take me to work with him for the entire day. Pay me a dollar, which is considerably below the union minimum. But I never ratted on him.

Eight years old. A tough time to be happy. I had just figured out there wasn't any Santa Claus and I had yet to discover sex. That leaves a real void in your life.

At this point in my life, total joy is a double chocolate milk shake. You know, the kind they serve in those big metal containers. Rarely can I get my parents to spring for one. But when my dad isn't with Ma, he's different. A pushover, if you will.

One day, I'm off from school—I think it was Columbus Day—and Dad takes me to work with him.

We get to the plant at four in the morning. Then it takes us two hours just to load up the truck. We spend the next ten or eleven hours driving all over the city, running into stores with boxes of potato chips. This particular day, around noon, we stop for a bite to eat. We're sitting at this little lunch counter and my dad says to me, "So, what do you want? Hamburger? grilled cheese?"

I figure, why not go for it. We're so far from home Ma will never hear me. "Gee, I don't know . . . I think I'll have . . . a double chocolate milk shake?"

My dad says to me, "Okay."

Okay? No begging? No pleading? Just "Okay."

Dad was a fun guy.

A few minutes later, I'm sloshed. It feels like double chocolate milk shake is oozing out of my ears. Then Dad speaks those immortal words to me. Words that show me there are no limits to the horizons of human happiness. Words that open up an entire universe of pleasure. My dad says to me, "Would you like another?"

Another? I had never even thought about the possibility. My mind could barely comprehend one double chocolate milk shake much less "another." I say, "Sure."

So I throw up ten minutes later. A small price to pay.

That night, I can't even eat dinner. Ma just thinks I'm tired. Dad doesn't rat on me either. We're pals.

At one of the stores where we had made a delivery, the owner had given me a pack of comic books. I am going to give half of them to Paul Godding because I want to use his new bat. Ma makes me give them to Danny instead. She gives me the old "your friends come and go but you only have one brother" routine.

There were times when sitting on this porch was the last thing in the world I wanted to do.

I am fifteen and Danny is twelve. I am young for my school year so almost all my friends turn sixteen before I do. Therefore, they get to drive before I do. It seems that all of them make it a point to drive by the house at least ten times a day.

I can, of course, ride along with any one of them. If he feels like it. If his girlfriend isn't available. If he has nothing better to do. Even then, I'm still just a passenger, going to places I'd rather not go and listening to radio stations I didn't choose.

In this neighborhood, few kids have their own rooms. The only privacy you get is in the bathroom, and even that isn't guaranteed during the morning rush. But with a driver's license, you have something better than your own room, if only for a few hours.

You have a room you can drive away from the house. The only way your mother or father can come knocking on the door is if they can run alongside at sixty miles an hour.

Sitting on the front porch literally watching my world roll by. Danny is sitting on the step above me. He is not welcomed. All I can think of is driving. Powering around in two thousand pounds of plea sure. Danny is twelve years old, for God's sake. He is still mailing away to Battle Creek, Michigan, for Kellogg toys.

"Get out of here," I snap.

"You don't own the porch."

"Just get the hell out of here," I yell.

"Nice language. That's a fine example you're setting for your younger brother." A direct Ma quote.

An old lady, in a brand-new car, crawls by at about seven miles an hour.

"Where's the justice?" I ask no one.

"Yeah," echoes Danny, "where's the justice?"

I can't tell if he is mocking me or agreeing with me. Not that I care either way. I ignore him.

"What does she need a car for anyway?" I say to no one. "Where does she have to go? To the store a couple of times a week for food? She's probably too fat already. Besides, old people don't hardly eat anything.

"Maybe visit a few friends? She should walk to see them. At that age, exercise is good for you."

"Right," chimes in Danny. "Right, right, right."

I glare over my shoulder and yell at him, "Shut up, will you?" and then return to my monologue.

"And look how slowly she drives," I say. "Although I can understand that," I reply sympathetically as I carry on both ends of the conversation, "at her age, the reflexes are gone.

"Why not a law," I ask myself, "where, when you reach sixty-five, maybe even fifty-five, you've got to give your license, and your car, to a sixteen-year-old—no, a fifteen-year-old? Makes sense to me.

"Taking their cars away from them would be for their own protection. Most of them are afraid to really get out there and drive. I mean, I do feel sorry for old people. It must be tough losing your reflexes and all."

Danny gets up from the porch. "I feel even sorrier for fifteen-year-olds. It must be tougher losing your brains."

10

Telling myself that I'd better get back into the house and start looking for that brown box. Ma's probably called two or three times since I've been gone.

Getting up from the step and walking through the front door again. Twice in twenty years. I'm getting good at this.

As I reenter the living room, I realize that I'm biting my fingernails, a nervous habit that's become considerably worse during the hours I've tried to quit smoking.

Remembering what Ma had said to me about it six weeks ago when she was visiting me in L.A. "Don't put your fingers in your mouth. You don't know where they've been."

Thinking it but not saying it. Why, Ma? Have you seen them going places without me?

When I was a kid, Ma was always saying things to me that made sense only to Ma. "If you're lost, ask someone for directions. But don't talk to strangers." When I was a little kid taking a bath, Ma would often shout up the stairs, "Wash yourself but don't touch yourself."

Feeling a little more relaxed about being back home now. I sit down on the edge of Dad's easy chair, which faces the television, and put the spiral notebook down on the floor beside me. A few years ago, I wrote some scripts for a family sitcom. They're so phony.

I wrote an early-morning scene and the producer told me that I had to show the men walking around the house in their pajamas. Right. Everybody knows that real men walk around in their underwear.

All the men in my family were real men. In fact, if Ma bought somebody a pair of pajamas, they knew they were on their way to the hospital.

I am fourteen and Danny's eleven. One night, we're watching the news. "We had our class election today," Danny says.

"Who won?" Like I care.

"Louis Sterkosky. He's a real jerk. He's going to do nothing but get us in trouble with the teacher."

"How did he get elected?"

"Most of the kids didn't care that much who won and the ones who did care convinced the rest of them to vote for Sterkosky."

"The majority's right," I say.

Danny quickly corrects me. "No, no, no. The majority rules. In fact, from what I can tell, the majority's almost always wrong. At one time, most people believed the world was flat but that didn't make it true."

"Whatever," I say disinterestedly as I try to end the conversation.

"The problem with political power," Danny explains, "is that the very kids who want it shouldn't have it while the kids who should have it don't want it."

I respond with silence hoping Danny will get the hint. He doesn't.

"Billy Dupson should be the class president."

"Why?" I pack as much exasperation and finality into one word as I can.

"Billy Dupson," Danny explains, "is basically a nice guy and he's also very big and strong. So even when he isn't nice, the rest of the class will convince themselves that he is."

I tell him, "Thomas Jefferson would be ashamed of you."

"Who cares what that mope thinks? They held him back last year."

When we are in our teens, Danny and I have this weekly ritual. Every Sunday morning, we get up early, make some popcorn, and watch those religious shows. You know, the crazy ones.

One morning we're watching the preacher going up and down the aisle curing people. All of a sudden, he turns to the camera and screeches, "Those of you at home who have arthritis in your hands, place them on the television and I will heal you."

Danny looks at me and says, "Kind of makes you wonder what you'd have to do if you had hemorrhoids, doesn't it?"

Right there, over the couch, there used to be a big mirror. I'd always check myself out in it before I went on a date.

Mirrors.

* * *

Nine months after the storm, Brian is born, just after sunrise, on a blue-eyed, color-in-your-cheeks, January day. The doctor says it is the easiest birth he has ever seen. Brian had come out so easily. From the very first moment, like all great actors, Brian moved instinctively toward the light.

As Brian is graduating from the high chair to a regular seat, he consistently chooses to sit directly across from me. I am flattered until I realize that the choice is not based on my personal magnetism but rather because of the mirror that hangs on the wall behind me.

Brian often stands or kneels on his plastic booster chair and delivers his performance. Although his words are aimed at me, his eyes and gestures are directed at the mirror. Occasionally, he makes brief eye contact with me. Already, he is learning to play to the front row.

Melinda and I repeatedly tell Brian to sit down and he does. But a few minutes later, he's back up again.

Now, I realize that Brian wasn't deliberately disobeying. He simply had to stand up to his passion.

Mirrors.

One Friday night, Danny and I stay up late to watch a movie. I am already out of high school and Danny is a junior. After we turn off the television, we realize that it has started to snow. The first snowfall of the year. Danny and I sit here and watch it snow and talk about very important things, which like most important things, have long since been forgotten.

A few weeks later, I find an essay on the kitchen table that Danny has written for his English class. The assignment is that you have to write about the first time something happens.

Danny writes about that snowfall. He writes about how gently the flakes fell with no wind to hurry them along. How there was no color, just the black of the sky, the grays of the earth, and the white of the snow. He titles his essay, "The First Silent Movie of the Season."

Then Danny goes on and writes about how, although there's always a first time for everything, there's always a last time, too.

He writes about how, when he was "growing up," he'd make faces in the bathroom mirror. He'd even practice kissing on it. But one day, he decides that he's too old for that kind of stuff so he makes one more face, gives it one last kiss, and that's it.

I am shocked, not by what he's written—we've all done that silly stuff—but who would admit it?

There are no family photos in the living room or, I suspect, anywhere else in the house. There used to be. Don't know why. Perhaps Ma's like me. Cameras have memories that are a little too accurate.

A few years ago, I'm visiting Brian at his mother's house. He wants to go through the family album, so we do. There are pages of pictures of him as an infant and then as a young child and I am in virtually none of them.

"See, Dad," he says, "even when you lived with us you were never around."

"Brian, who do you think was taking the pictures?"

Walking into the kitchen. Still hungry. Finishing the bottle of pop I'd left on the table.

Noticing a spot of dried glue. One night, after one of my birthdays, I'm sitting at the table trying to glue together a model airplane. My grandmother,

Dad's ma naturally, had given it to me. That was before anyone knew the effects of that glue.

Grandma calls to see how the plane's coming. "Well, Grandma," I say, "the plane's not doing so well but I'm gaining altitude."

Noticing a French cookbook on the counter. I don't think Ma's ever tasted French food in her life, but she's always loved to read the books.

I meet Rita for the first time in a French restaurant. It's the kind of place where when you ask for a glass of water, they give it a three-syllable name, drop a slice of lemon in it, and charge you.

The moment I sit down, I go to light up a cigarette, but Rita, who has made the reservation, points out that we're sitting in a nonsmoking section.

Rita's the new publicist for Tommy Tyler, one of the young up and coming comedians for whom I've been writing. Her basic mission is to see if I can turn his style from nightclub crass into television class.

Just before I had left my apartment, I had been on the phone with Ma. She had been complaining about how lonely it was to cook for just one person. I guess I was still thinking about that.

"You know, when I was a kid," I say to Rita, "my family almost never went to a restaurant. When we did, Ma would spend half the meal complaining about the food and we'd all agree."

"Your mother was a wonderful cook, Mr. Cooper?"

"Her cooking was fine. But it just wouldn't have been a good idea to disagree with her when she was criticizing somebody else's cooking, if you know what I mean."

The menu is in French. Handing it back to the waiter, I say, "I can only eat in one language. I'll have a steak, medium, baked potato with extra sour cream on the side, and green beans. Overcook them if you can."

The waiter opens the menu and looks through it incredulously. "That is on the menu, Monsieur?"

"No, but I'm sure it's in the kitchen somewhere."

Rita orders something in French. Then she says, "I've heard wonderful things about this restaurant. *L.A.* magazine just gave it a rave review. The chef is especially gifted in haute cuisine."

"My tongue is rather ignorant, I'm afraid."

"What do you mean?" Rita asks.

"When I'm not hungry, the thought of food bores me. When I am hungry, I'll eat bricks."

"I see . . . Actually, Mr. Cooper, the reason I thought it would be a good idea to meet with you is that Mr. Tyler wants to be a television talk show host and we feel he could be a very good one. We also feel that you could be instrumental in helping Mr. Tyler achieve that goal."

"Tommy's a wonderful nightclub comedian," I say. "I suspect that he could be a great comedic actor. But a television talk show host has to have the ability to listen to his guests. Tommy won't even listen to me."

"Perhaps," says Rita, "but we're hoping to get interesting guests."

The dinner arrives. Rita has ordered something that is, basically, a large green salad. She gives my entree a slight look of disdain. "One of my new clients," she says, "is a psychologist who's written a wonderful book on nutrition. It's just changed my way of looking at food."

"Based on the stare you just gave mine, I think you could stand a change in the way you look at food."

"Do you realize," lectures Rita, "that experts say

if you eat right, drink right, exercise, and don't smoke, you could live an extra ten years."

I throw some extra sour cream on my baked potato. "Let me tell you something about those extra ten years. They're not giving you your twenties again. They're putting them on at the end. That's just ten more years at the nursing home, sitting under the quilt, waiting for those chest pains to come back. No, thanks. I think I'll just eat and drink like a pig and then get the hell out of here."

"Obviously."

The conversation is a continuous duel. Just before dessert, and then only briefly, we both lower our swords. Rita mentions that when she was a child she dreamed of being a novelist.

"What did you want to be when you were a child?" she asks me.

"Nothing in particular," I lie. I would have felt like a jerk telling her I had wanted to be a major-league baseball player. But then I tell her a truth. "But for quite a few years now, I've wanted to write a book, too."

"Really?"

"Honest to God," I tell her.

"Then why haven't you?" Rita asks.

"Well, you're the one who had the childhood dreams of being a novelist," I counter, "why haven't you?"

Rita says it quietly. "I don't have the talent. What's your excuse?"

"I don't know," I say. "I just can't think of anything important enough to write about."

"I have a friend," says Rita, "who's only thirty-three years old and she's just finished her fifth book."

I'm truly impressed. "I don't think I've read that many."

For dessert, Rita orders a fresh fruit yogurt and I order the triple chocolate mousse cake.

As the waiter walks away with our order, Rita says to me, "Do you know how much fat is in something like that?"

"You know what bothers me about yogurt?" I counter. "How do you know when it spoils? You can tell when other foods spoil. Milk, for instance. You can tell when that spoils. It's yogurt."

"Look," says Rita pointing to the menu, "they have carob cake."

"I don't like carrots."

"Not *carrot, carob*. It's very healthy for you and it tastes just like chocolate."

"Are you sure?" I ask.

"Positive," Rita assures me.

So the waiter brings me a piece of carob cake and places it in front of me.

"Trust me," says Rita. "Carob tastes just like chocolate."

I taste it. It doesn't.

Rita is offended. She says, "Well, at least it looks like chocolate."

"Hey, lots of things look like chocolate."

Rita concludes the evening by stating that I am boorish, abrasive, and arrogant. By the time I get back to my apartment, I conclude that she's right.

I call to apologize. By the end of the conversation, we have another date for dinner, but not at a French restaurant.

The phone rings. Automatically grabbing the spiral notebook, I go into the kitchen and pick up the receiver in mid ring.

"Hello, Ma—"

"Donald, you should not answer the phone that way. How did you know it was me?"

"Who else would it be?" I ask.

"This may come as a surprise to you, Donald, but I get many calls from many different people." Ma is perturbed.

"You're right, Ma. I shouldn't answer the phone that way."

"I've been calling for the past couple of hours. Where have you been?"

"I took a walk."

"Oh, then you've already found the brown box?"

"Ah . . . no . . ."

"It wasn't in the garage?" Ma asks.

"I haven't looked for it yet."

"Donald, you know how important that box is to me. You know how worried I am about it."

"Ma, I'll find it. I'll start looking for it right now."

"I really don't know what I'd do if it was lost . . ."

"I'll find it."

"I'm almost certain it's in the garage, just inside the door—"

"I'll check."

"You're not taking any more walks, are you?"

"No, Ma."

"And you'll call me as soon as you find it. You'll call me either way, won't you?"

"Yes, Ma . . ."

"And you'll—"

"Ma, I can't look for the box if I'm still on the phone."

"I'm depending on you, Donald."

"I'll find the box. Good-bye, Ma."

"Okay, good-bye."

Time to get out to the garage and find that damn box. Opening the back door and walking through the backyard. I am shocked at how small it is. Ma must have sold off a few acres. I try opening the garage door, but it won't budge. After a few hard kicks to the bottom, it finally pops open.

Switching on the light. A damp, musty odor permeates the air. Every inch of floor space is being fought over by, among others, boxes of nails, bags of old clothes, rusting lawn furniture, parts of an engine, a lawn mower, crippled bikes, and paint cans of all sizes.

I knew my parents would never get a divorce. My dad could never throw anything out. His joke. He only told it once.

I rest the spiral notebook on top of a carton of empty pop bottles and begin looking for the brown box. It's not "just inside the door" or anywhere near just inside the door. I continue to rummage through the crowd looking for the box.

About the only thing my dad never put in this garage was the car. One morning, just after he leaves for work, Ma decides that one way or the other, the car is going in this garage. She drags me out here, we spend all afternoon shoving everything to one side and then, somehow, she manages to pull in the car.

Just as she's doing it, my dad walks in here. The expression on his face is one of total shock. You would have thought he had just found the car in the middle of the kitchen. He says, "What the hell is the car doing in the garage?"

Damn! Catching my shirt on the edge of a saw. So far, no brown box.

The garage really became Danny's territory. When he's in sixth grade, he wants to learn how to play the trumpet. If you join the school band, you get a good rental deal, so Ma says okay. But we all insist that he practice here inside the garage. That's fine with Danny. He says he loves the way the trumpet sounds in here anyway.

About a year later, Danny decides to quit the band, which means he has to buy his own trumpet. Doesn't bother him. He goes out and gets a newspaper route to pay for it. One day I ask him, "Why did you quit the band?"

Danny says, "Because I can't hear myself play."

That's the strange thing about Danny and that trumpet. He never plays it for anybody. He's a very popular guy. Has a lot of friends and is always going places. For a while, if his friends are going to a party or a dance where they know the guys in the band, they ask him to bring along his trumpet. But he just never does. A group of his friends form a band and want him to join them, but he doesn't do that either.

The only one I know of that Danny ever plays that trumpet for is another kid named Danny who lives a few blocks over from here. This Danny kid is mildly retarded. He seems to spend a lot of his time walking, by himself, through the neighborhood alleys. A lonely kid. The kind that others avoid.

I'm walking past the garage one day and I hear Danny playing. I stick my head inside and there's this Danny kid just sitting there watching him.

Then Danny, my brother, gives the trumpet to this Danny kid who tries playing it. He's awful. My brother takes the trumpet back and starts playing his favorite song, which is, not surprisingly, "Oh, Danny Boy." Then my brother says to this Danny kid, "Now watch. The lips are strong. The fingers are gentle."

I always knew my brother was popular with the girls. But until that day I never knew why. But I'll tell you, Danny could sure play that trumpet.

* * *

For a moment, I think I see the brown box. Standing on a small table, stepping up onto a workbench, I reach up and take the box off a high shelf. But there's no top on the box and it's empty.

Noticing a pile of rags trapped between the big overhead door and a mob of paint cans. A fire waiting to happen. I take the empty box, climb down from the table, and work my way over to the overhead door.

After shoving all the rags into the box, I decide that the fastest way to the garbage cans, which are outside in the alley, is to simply open the overhead door.

Pushing against the lower part of the door, trying to get it to open. My dad would never buy an automatic garage door opener. He said he was raising two of them. Finally, the door starts giving way. With a final shove from me, its own momentum carries it up and over my head.

I walk over and toss the box of rags into one of the garbage cans.

Looking around. It occurs to me that I have not been in an alley, a real alley, since I left home twenty years ago. Kids like alleys. They're disorganized, smelly, and dirty. So are alleys.

If alleys were streets, they'd be a disaster. Kids love disasters. A flooded basement is a kid's private wading pool. A snowstorm that cripples the city gives a kid a free day so he has time to play in it.

If a teacher announces to the typical class, "Children, nuclear war has just begun and, within a few hours, the earth is going to be totally destroyed," a hand would immediately be raised. "Does this mean we get tomorrow off?"

Behind the garages, in the alley, is where you sneaked a smoke and talked about sex when you were fourteen years old. We could have talked about sex anywhere but it always seemed dirtier in the alley.

The sadness is that the average fourteen-year-old boy has a more active sex life when he's asleep than the average forty-year-old man does when he's awake. Now when I hear that a friend of mine's gotten lucky, I think of the lottery.

We certainly weren't taught anything in school about sex. I didn't learn in school, for instance, that the average male hits his sexual peak at seventeen. I didn't learn that until I was eighteen.

Women? Their early thirties. Which shows you that God does have a sense of humor. So when I was in high school, in the backseat of a car, and the girl was saying, "Not now," she was talking a good twelve, thirteen years.

One great thing about getting older, though, is having kids. Brian truly makes my life worth living even if he does want to be an actor.

Going back into the garage and spending another hour searching for the brown box. No luck. It's got to be in the basement.

Walking through the yard and onto the back porch. There are still deep marks on the bottom of the door where Blackie would scratch to get in. Dad barely tolerated that dog. He said he had no use for anyone who ran around the house naked and didn't use the bathroom. Of course, by those standards, for at least the first couple of years, he probably wasn't too fond of Danny or me.

Ma loved Blackie. She said that he was like one of the family. Dad said he looked like her side. That was another joke he only told once.

A few years ago, I wrote some material for a comedienne named Maggie Walters, a tiny, extremely nervous and vicious woman. In another life, she had been a Chihuahua. Maybe that's why she loved dog jokes.

Blackie was my inspiration. Maggie had an older sister named Hilary, whom she hated, naturally, so I'd work her into the material, too.

Stuff like, "We had a dog named Queenie. You'd open the freezer, ice cubes would fall out. She'd pick them up and hide them. We thought that was pretty stupid until we found out she was also hiding a bottle of Scotch." "If you own a big dog, you know this is true. She'd drink out of the toilet. Used to drive my older sister, Hilary, crazy. When she's thirsty, she hates to wait in line." "And when you walked in a room, she'd stick her nose in your crotch . . . not the dog, my older sister . . ."

Sitting around in my studio apartment, analyzing an average day in the life of my dead dog so I can write one-liners for a reborn Chihuahua. Not exactly brain surgery.

Walking through the kitchen and down the stairs into the basement. As Ma would be quick to point out, it's a "finished" basement as opposed to an "unfinished" one; paneling on the wall. Tile on the floor.

The Ping-Pong table, folded up, is pinned against the wall by a pair of bikes. Danny and I had some great games on that table. Usually, one of us would win by just a point. Did we feel like jerks when we found out you had to win by two.

I am thirteen and Danny is ten. He is a better player but I'm funnier. Sometimes I get him with my play-by-play. Since we both have the same last name it often gets confusing.

"Cooper hits one to Cooper's forehand and Cooper returns it down the sideline. Cooper answers that with a slice shot, which Cooper slams down the middle of the court but Cooper handles that with a lob right on the baseline but Cooper hits an overhead, which pulls Cooper out of position. Cooper is everywhere and Cooper just can't handle it . . .''

I am, indeed, the funnier one. Small solace.

I am sixteen and Danny's thirteen. We are at a church outing and we are playing softball at a picnic grove, which is about a thirty-minute drive from the neighborhood. I've told Danny that we can only stay for part of the game because I have to drive back to the neighborhood park to play in a league game later in the afternoon. I'm almost playing first string.

I can tell that Danny wants to stay for the entire picnic. He's having a great time. But he knows that I'd never, ever skip one of my games so he doesn't even bother arguing.

There is a forest preserve in deep left field. Before Danny bats, a couple of other players hit balls that drive the outfielders to the edges of the trees.

Danny steps up to the plate. Since he's only thirteen, the outfielders play him rather shallow. The pitcher lobs the ball up to the plate. It appears that Danny's going to allow the pitch to go past him. At the last instant, hardly moving, but with incredible speed, he swings the bat off his shoulder and it explodes into the ball. The left fielder hardly has a chance to move before the ball rockets over his head and disappears beyond the tops of the front row of trees.

When Danny comes up to bat again, the outfielders, naturally, play him deeper. But the infielders also take a few big steps backward. Their movements seem to be motivated less by strategy and more by self preservation.

I haven't seen Danny play baseball in a long time, mainly because he hasn't played in a long time, and I am astounded.

Until that day, Paul Godding has been the most powerful hitter I have ever personally seen. His is a brutal act. He doesn't so much swing at the ball as hack his way through it. But Danny's motion is truly a swing. The difference between watching someone wielding an ax or a magic wand.

We stay for the entire picnic.

Gazing. The basement is strewn with pieces of my family's life: Baby clothes, schoolbooks, bags of sweaters, toys, photo albums, a retired radio. Born and bought with enthusiasm. But as the years have sifted them through our lives and our home, they have finally come to rest, old and faded, in the basement.

Including some dreams.

I see them loitering in the corner, a bat with a baseball cap sitting atop its head and my glove lounging beside them.

Taking the cap off the bat and placing it on a stool. Wrapping my fist around the handle of the bat, gently swinging it as if getting ready for the next pitch. This is the last bat I ever bought. I was eighteen years old.

Eighteen years old. Paul Godding is playing better baseball than ever. Warren, like most of the other guys in the neighborhood, had quit playing years ago. But I'm still playing rotten and still thinking I have a chance of making it to the major leagues. What a dreamer.

Right here, in this basement, is where the dream ended.

Over there, in the corner, we used to have an

old television. One day, I'm watching the ball game. The announcer says, "The hitter checks his swing." A simple statement. I'd heard it a million times before. But, for some reason that day I suddenly realize what the man is saying.

Even on the low level of baseball I'm playing, I can barely see the ball go by me. Now here's this guy in the majors. The ball's coming at him at over ninety miles an hour. It's curving, sliding, hooking. It takes two-tenths of a second for the ball to get from the pitcher's mound to the plate.

In two-tenths of a second, this guy not only has time to decide on whether or not to swing, he has time to change his mind. He reconsiders. He checks his swing. In two-tenths of a second.

That August, Paul Godding is signed by the Detroit Tigers to a minor league contract and goes to Florida to play on one of their teams. Warren starts college at the state university. I get a job in a shoe store. You know, shoes, for your feet. With my grades, I'm lucky I get the job in the shoe store.

Putting the bat down. Slipping on the glove. Punching the pocket. Smelling the leather. Reliving the night I went over to Paul Godding's house to say good-bye.

Dusk. My legs have to push my body through the hot August air. When I get over there, his dad is out in front putting luggage in the trunk. Paul's parents are driving him down to Florida the next morning.

Paul is in his bedroom, stuffing underwear and his baseball equipment, his gloves, his spikes, into a duffel bag.

"Hey, Godding," I say as I walk into his room. "I want to make sure I get an autograph before the line gets too long."

"You're a funny guy," says Paul. He means it literally.

Paul Godding has many other things going for him, but a sense of humor is not one of them. Whenever I make a smart-ass remark to Paul, which is rare since he is such a rotten audience, he almost always says, "You're a funny guy." It has never occurred to him, however, that not once has he ever laughed at anything I've said.

"I may be funny, but you're the one heading for the majors," I say.

"It's only Double A ball," replies Paul. " 'The big top' is still a long way away."

Baseball people sometimes refer to the major leagues as "the big top."

"I'm hoping they'll promote me to Triple-A next year," says Paul. "Two years after that, I should be in the majors. If it takes a couple more years than I figure, I'll still only be twenty-three my rookie year. A major-league player doesn't hit his prime until his late twenties."

"You see," I say, "that's why I'm lucky to be in the business I'm in. A shoe salesman doesn't peak until his early seventies."

"That's interesting," says Paul. "I didn't know that."

In the past couple of years, I have noticed that unless Paul and I are talking about baseball, we really aren't talking at all.

"I'm going to try and get them to take a look at me in the outfield," says Paul. "I think I can get to the big top a lot faster as an outfielder. You think that's a good idea?"

"Yeah," I say. "I think it's a very good idea." We have had this conversation at least twenty times in the past week.

Paul has been signed up to play first base. But there is a problem with being a young first baseman. Sometimes, the parent team has a great hitter whose age is robbing him of the agility to field his position. The team will often move him over to first base since that position doesn't require much fielding range.

"So you really think it would be a good idea, my playing the outfield?"

"Yeah. Look, I've got to get going. I have a lot to do myself tonight." In fact, according to my calendar, I have the rest of my life free.

We shake hands. "Good luck, Paul. I know you're going to make it."

"I know I will," he says calmly. He means it, too.

Walking out the door. "Write," I say. "Let me know how you're doing."

"I will."

He doesn't.

As I walk up to my house, I see a rubber ball on the lawn. Throwing it against the steps. It catches the edge and goes sailing over my head. Feeling really lousy.

Getting up early the next morning, I go to my bedroom window and look across the street. The Godding car is gone.

Slowly searching the basement for the brown box, I find a little white box filled with greeting cards, little notes and letters that Donna Trandelli had sent me in junior high and high school. She had sent me plenty more than these. I guess the rest have gotten lost with time. I sent as many to her, probably more.

Two weeks after Paul Godding leaves town, Donna Trandelli dumps me, too. We had dated all through high school. Had even talked about getting married. But I had only brought up the subject late at night, if you know what I mean.

Since our graduation in June, two of her girl-friends had become engaged. Another was expecting a ring on her birthday in a few weeks. Not good. Donna was enrolled in secretarial school for the fall.

We are sitting on her front porch. Her older sister is married now and has two children.

"Donald," Donna asks, "what do you plan on doing in the fall?"

"I don't know. I'm working in the shoe store."

"You can't do that forever."

"I don't know," I say. "When I'm at the store, it seems like I've been doing it forever."

"Donald, what plans do you have for the future? Solid plans."

Solid. Donna is not looking for philosophical speculations.

"I don't know . . ."

"Well," she says, "you're eighteen years old. You should know."

"I don't know . . . something exciting . . . something different . . ."

"What?" Donna says it quite emphatically.

"I don't know."

"My father says you're just a dreamer."

"Well . . . you see—"

"Actually, he doesn't say that," Donna says. "I was trying to spare your feelings. He says you're a bum."

"You know, Donna, there's quite a distance between dreamer and bum."

"My father can get you a job at the steel plant, in his office."

"Gee, I don't think so. . . ."

"He's been there twenty-nine years."

"God, I really—"

"Donald, I like that kind of security."

"I don't think it would be a good idea to work in the same office as your father."

"Why not? Oh, I know he isn't very fond of you now, but once you really know each other—"

"That's not it," I say. "Let's say your dad gets me a job. In a few years, because I'm so bright, hardworking, and just a darn decent guy, they make me the boss of the whole office. Then word comes down from headquarters that I have to unload some of the dead weight. . . ."

Donna Trandelli decides to unload her dead weight right then and there.

Looking again at the bat propped up in the corner. Eighteen years old. In senior year of high school, when Brian is eighteen, he plays Willie Loman in *Death of a Salesman* and I believe him. A year later, in college, he plays the lead role in *Peter Pan* and I believe him again.

Brian approaches each role with all the enthusiasm, intensity, and dedication of a scholar to his work.

At first, his talent shocks me. Then it awes me. Then it scares me.

With Paul Godding and Donna Trandelli out of my life, I find myself spending a lot more time with Danny. As the two of us have gotten older, the three-year difference in our ages no longer seems to be the great barrier it once was. Now I don't mind him tagging along although he doesn't want to as much as he once did. I actually look forward to doing things with Danny.

My dreams of playing professional baseball are dead but I still enjoy going to the park and "hitting 'em out" just to relax. Now Danny comes along with me. When Danny feels like going to the mall, he'll usually ask me to join him and I will.

The brown box is not here. Everything's beginning to get to me. I just want to get the hell out of this house.

I can't believe it. The damn phone's ringing again. Waiting. Maybe it'll stop. It doesn't. Stomping up the stairs to the kitchen.

"Hello."

"What's wrong with you?" Ma asks.

"Nothing."

"You sound like you're upset about something."

"I'm not upset about anything."

"You certainly sound like something's bothering you."

Very slowly. "I am not upset."

"The phone must have rung twenty times. Were you out taking another walk?"

"No, Ma."

"I'm sure it rang at least twenty times. . . ."

"I was in the basement, Ma, looking for the damn box."

"I don't appreciate that kind of language."

"The box isn't down there."

"I told you to look in the garage first."

"I did, Ma. It's not there either."

"You're positive it's not in the garage?"

"Positive. The damn place is so messy."

"I don't want to hear you talking that way about your father."

"I didn't say anything about my father."

Ma says, "Then the brown box has to be in the upstairs bedroom."

"Ma, I told you I don't want to go up there. Look, it's getting late. I know you don't want Aunt Claire coming over here but—"

"It has to be in the upstairs bedroom."

I persist. "I can't see why Aunt Claire or maybe one of the neighbors—"

"Donald, you're not listening to me. I'm sure it's in the upstairs bedroom."

"Ma, you're not listening to me. I told you I don't want to go up there."

"That's silly. There's nothing to be afraid of."

"I didn't say there was anything to be afraid of. I just don't want to go up there."

"Donald, you know how important that box is to me."

"I know, Ma, but—"

"I've sat here all day worrying about it. I can't think of anything else."

"All right, all right, I'll go look, for Christ's sake."

"Stop that swearing."

"That's not swearing," I say.

"As far as I'm concerned, it is."

"Okay, it is swearing."

"Now you'll call me as soon as you find the box?"

"Yeah, Ma."

"You won't forget?"

"Ma, I said I will call you right away."

"You won't be taking any more walks?"

"No, Ma. I've got to go . . ."

"You know what the box looks like?"

"Yes. I've got to go. Good-bye."

"Good-bye."

Leaning against the counter. I am exhausted. God, what I'd do for a cigarette. Remembering the two "emergency" ones in my shirt pocket. Looking at my watch. Two o'clock, Chicago time. In only two hours now, I can make the call and get the results of the biopsy. If the news is bad, wondering how I'll deal with it.

* * *

I am fifteen and Danny is twelve. One of his class-mates dies suddenly from a viral infection.

That night, lying in our beds waiting for sleep. "Boy, that's scary," I say as I snap my fingers. "Some-body dying just like that."

"Dying can't be that difficult," replies Danny. "I've never heard of anyone who couldn't do it."

Taking a cigarette out of my pocket and rolling it be-tween my fingers. What difference can one cigarette make now? Rummaging through the junk drawer and finding a pack of matches.

I decide to call Rita. Talking to her always re-vives my spirits. But her secretary informs me that Rita's out of town for the next few days. I've forgot-ten about that goofy family reunion in Akron.

Walking into the living room and looking up at the staircase. It always seemed darker than the rest of the house.

When I was a little kid, especially at night, I was afraid of it. I always had the same nightmare where I started walking up it but midway a myste-rious force stopped me and I spent the rest of my life there, standing in the dark in the middle of the stairs.

I sit down on the edge of my dad's easy chair and begin to light the cigarette. Then I remember. Walking out onto the front porch, my legs ease the rest of me down to the top of the first step. No one's allowed to smoke in the house.

Lighting up. Taking a long, deep drag. It tastes almost harsh. Maybe it needs a cup of coffee and a donut.

I feel sorry for Ma, growing old. It's tough, let-ting go. Sometimes, when it's your own parent, this kind of thing sort of sneaks up on you.

No one, not even Ma, wants to admit they're getting older.

A few months ago, Ma calls me in L.A. She had just returned from her cousin's wake. He was ninety-one years old. Ma says to me, "You know, in today's world, ninety-one isn't really that old."

I don't say anything to Ma but I'm thinking it. Isn't old? Ma, if he was a coin, he'd be worth a few hundred bucks.

Then Ma says to me, "He looked so much better at the funeral home than he did in the hospital."

Yeah, right, Ma. Well, maybe they should have brought him there first. What do you think?

Get old and the world runs you over. When I was a little kid, Ma would take me to visit her aunt, my great aunt Bernice, who lived in a downtown high rise on the fifteenth floor. Aunt Bernice was somewhere in her eighties.

After one of our visits, Ma and I are standing at the elevator. I read that sign: IN CASE OF FIRE, USE THE STAIRCASE.

Even my child's mind realizes the idiocy of the situation. My Aunt Bernice stands a better chance of surviving by jumping out the window than walking down fifteen flights of stairs. I had seen her blow two weeks just crossing the living room.

Glancing at my watch again. Getting late. Might as well get it over with. Rubbing the cigarette out on the step, I reach for my spiral notebook but then decide to leave it here. No one will bother it.

Pushing myself up, I open the front door, take a few steps into the living room and then begin climbing the stairs to the second floor. Midway up the staircase, I pause for a moment and wonder what it would be like to spend the rest of my life there.

Each step groans and crackles under my weight.

When I was a kid I knew, just by listening, who was traveling on them. Giant groans and loud crackles meant Dad was on the stairs. An occasional groan and rapid-fire crackles announced Ma's footsteps. Danny's footsteps ignited only light, sporadic crackles.

I walk down the hallway and step into the bedroom. There used to be two beds here.

I am nine and Danny's six. One morning, he's jumping up and down on the bed as high as he can get. I walk in the door and Ma's right behind me. She gives him a few whacks on the behind. Very unusual as Danny doesn't ordinarily misbehave . . . and when he does, he doesn't get caught.

Now Ma's even sorry she's hit him. She says, "Danny, what would you do if you were a mother and you caught your little boy jumping up and down on the bed?"

Through his sniffles Danny says, "I'd buy that poor kid a trampoline."

When Danny was a child, he would wage a nightly war against falling asleep. One evening, even though it's early, Danny is staggering around. Dad says to him, "You're tired. Go to bed."

Danny defiantly replies, "I am not tired."

Dad says, "You're either tired or drunk. Either way, you're out of here."

Many years later, Danny discovered the difference.

I am eighteen and Danny's fifteen. Late one Friday night, I'm sitting in the living room watching television when Danny walks in through the front door. He looks as if he has been trapped in an accordion and his feet are moving as if they are playing a very slow, and very sloppy, game of hopscotch.

"You look terrible," I say.

"Thank you, Clark Gable."

Danny begins trudging up the stairs.

"No, I'm serious. You feel all right? You look like you've got the flu or something."

Danny mumbles a few words I can't understand as he continues climbing up the stairs.

I walk back into the kitchen where Ma and Dad are both sitting at the table. "Something's wrong with Danny," I announce. "He looks pretty sick to me."

Both of them get up and head upstairs with me tagging along behind. When we all walk into the bedroom, Danny is lying on top of his bed, staring up at the ceiling. His mouth is hanging open. His breathing is deliberate.

"He really looks sick." Dad sounds worried.

"I think it's the flu," I say.

Ma says, "He's drunk."

Dad and I look at each other. Of course, that's it. Once you think in those terms, it is rather obvious. Danny is blasted.

I am stunned and somewhat delighted. Danny has always been the ideal son. I, on the other hand, have come from the factory with a number of flaws.

"What were you drinking?" says Dad in a demanding tone of voice.

"Beer . . . just beer."

"How many beers did you have?"

"Ah . . . let me think . . . six . . . six . . ."

"Six six-packs," I say. "That's a lot of beer."

Dad gives me a disgusted look. "I do not want to hear any of your silly crap now, got it?"

"Got it."

He returns his attention to Danny. "Who sold you that beer? Because when I get a hold of that guy—"

Ma begins walking out of the bedroom. "Who cares who sold it to him? There are always temptations out there. He's responsible for his actions."

Dad stops talking to Danny and follows Ma out of the room and I can hear them shouting at each other as they go down the stairs. They aren't exactly arguing with each other. I think they're debating about the best way to kill him. I throw another sneer at Danny, but his eyes are too glazed over to notice.

Later, when I go up to bed, the room doesn't exactly smell like a flower shop so I sleep on the living-room couch. During the night, I keep hearing Danny getting up and going to the bathroom.

The next morning, I'm sitting at the table eating breakfast when Danny trudges into the kitchen. He stumbles around the room for a few minutes as he prepares his breakfast.

"You know," I say to him, "you're walking like Grampa." Danny mumbles an obscenity under his breath. Finally, he sits down with a piece of toast and a cup of tea, hardly his usual morning fare.

"Great," I say. "Now you're walking like Grampa and eating like Grandma."

"Shove it." That's not exactly what he says but it's close enough.

After Danny leaves for work, Mrs. Henderson comes to the door demanding to see Ma. Her kid hangs around with Danny and apparently he had come home drunk last night, too. She refuses to enter the house, choosing instead to stand on the porch.

"I'm very disappointed in Daniel," says Mrs. Henderson to Ma. "I've allowed my Harold to keep company with Daniel because I've believed that Daniel would be a positive influence. Now, this happens."

Ma says nothing.

"Obviously," continues Mrs. Henderson, "your son isn't the Mr. Perfect everyone thinks he is."

"You're wrong," replies Ma as she swings the door shut. "Last night, Danny was the perfect drunk."

Danny, an incredibly light sleeper. He once whined to Ma that I was making too much noise with my blankets. Danny's usual routine was that for the first hour after he'd go to bed, he would get up about every ten minutes to complain about all the noises that were keeping him awake.

The rest of us would be sitting in the living room watching television and Danny, dragging a blanket or a pillow, would come down the stairs and announce, "How can a guy get any sleep around here with you playing that television so loud?"

I'd often go to bed after Danny did. I'd come in here and the moment I turned on the light, Danny would sit up in his bed and yell, "For God's sake, I'm trying to sleep."

One night I come in and turn on the light and nothing happens. Apparently, the bulb had burned out. Regardless, Danny bolts up in his bed and yells, "For God's sake, I'm trying to sleep."

"What the hell are you talking about? There's no light on."

"It's the noise of the switch. It's deafening."

There was one night where when we got home we both had trouble sleeping.

I am seventeen and Danny's fourteen. A hot August evening where the humidity is so heavy even the air has trouble breathing. Danny and I are driving down a two-lane highway in the middle of central Illinois. Endless stalks of corn are running by both sides of us. All the windows are rolled down but not even the wind has the energy to jump in.

Danny asks, "How much farther is it?"

Just then, a sign appears: JOLANO, 12 MILES. I say, "Oh, twelve miles?"

Danny either doesn't get it or doesn't care to.

Earlier that evening, he had gotten a call, collect, from that Danny kid who had told Danny that he caught a bad cold and was now in the hospital's health facility. He asked Danny if he could visit him tonight and bring down some things he needed. According to Danny, the kid really sounded sad. Danny had filled up a duffel bag with some books, toiletries, sweat shirts, and jeans and then asked my dad if he'd drive him.

I quickly volunteered. Dad was not enthusiastic about giving me the car for that long a trip, especially at night. I had only had my license four months. But Dad was even less enthusiastic about making the trip himself.

As we drive along, Danny's spirits seem shrouded, but I'm in a great mood. Although it's only three hours from Chicago, Jolano is, by far, the longest trip for which Dad has allowed me to take the car. Besides, I don't get out much. Even going to a small town like Jolano is a bit of an adventure. And, of course, it's the first time I'll be visiting a mental hospital. In fact, the mental hospital complex is, by far, the largest one in the state and is Jolano's only claim to fame.

Danny's mood is beginning to depress me. "Jolano," I say, "I wonder what the city motto is. 'You'd have to be crazy not to come to Jolano, but then, you'd have to be crazy if you did.' 'Jolano, the Almond Joy of Illinois. We have lots of nuts, too.' 'Psycho—you've seen the movie. Now visit the town.' "

Danny doesn't even bother looking at me. "You're a sick guy, you know that?"

"Then I'm heading in the right direction, aren't I? You know what I bet people never say in Jolano? 'Hey, I'm as sane as the next guy.' "

A few minutes later, a 45, a 35, and then a 30 speed limit sign announce the arrival of Jolano. A typical small town—angled parking, a little movie house, a few empty stores, and too many taverns.

As we are beginning to drive out of town, a small green sign with an arrow pointing to a side road discreetly points out the way to Jolano State Hospital.

Turning. Within a few hundred yards, a heavy fog has fallen on us, throwing the night out of focus. I can barely see ahead of me. I say the obvious. "This is weird." The fog dissolves as suddenly as it had arrived.

A herd of barracklike buildings appear on our right. There is a guardhouse at the main entrance, a sign of a very wealthy housing development or a mental institution.

The guard looks at his clipboard. We've been expected. He tells us to drive straight ahead as far as we can, make a left, and then drive again as far as we can. The last building on our left will be the hospital.

A week earlier, Danny had been out collecting money from his newspaper customers. The Danny kid had tagged along to "help out." After the kid had asked repeatedly, Danny had allowed him to go up to a house and collect the monthly payment.

When the woman came to the door, the Danny kid, in his unique way, told her he wanted some money. He didn't bother mentioning anything about the newspapers.

The woman was a bit strange herself. She freaked and called the police. Even though Danny explained that the kid was just helping him out, the woman still had the Danny kid arrested for disturbing the peace.

The Danny kid's parents decided that their son needed some reevaluations and had him committed for observation. According to Danny, my brother, this happened fairly often. It was their way of getting a few weeks of free baby-sitting.

Once we enter it, Danny and I can see that the hospital is little more than simply another barrack in which the interior walls have been knocked down so that all that remains is one huge room.

Hospital beds seem to be randomly scattered throughout it. Just inside the door, an older, dignified man, wearing a somber face and dressed in state-issued pajamas, bathrobe, and slippers, is quietly singing nonsense syllables.

In another bed, a young boy, at least I think it's a boy, about twelve years old, lies sleeping beneath a thin sheet. Although his head and shoulders appear to be normal, the contours of the sheets suggest that there is very little else to his body.

We spot the Danny kid sitting on the end of a bed in the middle of the room. He is staring intently at us as if, by the power of his eyes alone, we will be drawn to him. It takes us a few moments of weaving around a maze of beds to get to him.

The Danny kid says hello to me and asks Danny what's in the duffel bag. Before he can answer, the kid starts apologizing for calling him tonight, for being in the hospital, for not getting the money from the lady, for not . . .

I talk over him and tell Danny that it's so hot in here . . . it really is . . . that I'm going outside to have a cigarette and that I'll wait for him there. Danny simply nods while he continues to listen to the ramblings of the kid.

Retracing my route around the beds and heading for the doors. Above them is a large clock with a sweeping second hand. You may not know where you are but at least you know exactly what time it is where you don't know where you are.

Standing outside smoking a cigarette. A few dozen feet in front of the hospital, the cornfields begin again. The fog is descending again. In the time it takes to smoke a couple of cigarettes, the stalks have their heads in the clouds.

Getting impatient. Stepping back into the hospital. Danny's walking toward me. The empty duffel bag is hanging from his hand.

"Let's go," said Danny. "He's asleep."

I look past Danny toward the Danny kid's bed. Even though I'm quite a distance from him, I see something large glimmering on his nightstand. At first, I think it's a bedpan.

A few minutes later, back on the two-lane highway, running through the lightless gamut of cornfields, I realize what it was. A trumpet.

* * *

On the wall here in the bedroom, between the windows there used to be a large poster of a white convertible with two perfect young women in it. They are driving along a perfect country road on a perfectly perfect day. Danny had written on the side of the car *"The Fortune."* The poster featured an exact model of The Fortune.

Danny had found the poster in a used-book store. He had been searching for it for months. He gave it to me as a gift. No occasion. He just gave it to me. My favorite all-time gift.

I am eighteen and Danny's fifteen. I have finally saved enough money to buy my own car. During my six months of used-car-lot browsing, I have seen a few convertibles I really like. The problem is, I know nothing about cars. The man who does, Dad, is in bed with an infection.

My dad can look at a car and, even if it isn't running, he can tell you what's wrong with it. I'd be doing well if I could tell what color it is.

Standing in his bedroom. "Gee, Dad, you look pretty healthy to me."

"The doc says that it'll be at least another two weeks before I can get out of bed. Look, I know you're anxious to buy a car, but I can't risk my life so that you can have wheels."

"Of course not, Dad." That's what I say but that's not what I'm thinking. Why not? If I was a father, I'd risk my life to get my son a car. After all, at eighteen, there is no life without a car. "It's just that I've seen a couple of convertibles that I really like."

"Take Danny. He knows cars."

"Danny? But he doesn't know cars the way you do."

"Then wait two weeks."

An hour later, Danny and I are at a used-car lot looking at one of the convertibles. Glaring at Danny, I feel like I've asked for the chief surgeon and gotten stuck with the butcher's assistant.

Danny walks around the car deliberately a few times with me following behind him. He is taking notes on a small pad of paper. "How much?" he asks the salesman.

What a stupid question, I think. The sign's right on the front of the car.

"The sign's right on the front of the car," the salesman says.

"How much for us?" asks Danny.

"I'll knock off ten percent," replies the salesman.

I am impressed.

Danny glides his hand along the side of a fender. "This car's been hit."

"Where?" asks the salesman.

"Right here," Danny points out. "It's been bonded."

I run my hand along the fender, too. "Hey, it has been bonded." Whatever the hell that is.

They both ignore me.

Danny looks at the bottom of a door. "Some rust spots."

"This is a used car," says the salesman.

Danny writes a number down on his pad and shows it to the salesman. "This is what we'll give you for it."

"No way," the salesman shouts. "The blue book value of this car is twice that."

"But that's for a car that hasn't been hit," replies Danny. "Besides, that value is based on an average mileage of twelve thousand a year and this car has averaged nearly twenty thousand miles."

"Well," says the salesman, "that's true. Look,

why don't we all take it for a test drive and talk
when we get back?''

I motion Danny into the backseat. Then I slide
behind the wheel while the salesman gets in on the
passenger's side.

Starting up the car. Danny taps me on the shoulder.

"Turn on the radio."

"I want to hear how the engine runs first," I say.
Like I'd know.

"Will you turn on the radio?" he persists, so I
do.

"Punch the buttons."

"Just tell me what station you want."

"I don't want any station. I just want you to
punch all the buttons."

So I do.

"Notice," says Danny, "they all land on rock
stations." Danny looks at me. "Buy another car."

Two days later, I do, paying half what the dealer
had been asking, but much more than I had planned
on spending. Even in my most expensive dreams, I
wasn't driving a car like this one, a white-on-white
convertible with an engine big enough for NASA to
envy.

When I'm standing there, debating, with my
checkbook in one hand and my pen in the other,
Danny says to me, "Remember, you're going to be
dead a long time."

"All right, all right." I start signing.

"We need a name," says Danny.

"This is a car, not a dog."

"It's more fun if it has a name."

"Then you name it," I say as I rip the check out
of the book. Looking at the check. "There goes the
fortune."

"That's a great name," says Danny. " 'The Fortune.' "

So it is.

A sunny, early summer day. Danny and I drive The Fortune up in front of the house so Dad can see it from the living-room window. He gives the thumbs-up sign. Ma comes out for a ride.

Danny and I think she'll get a kick out of sitting in the backseat. She doesn't.

"It's too windy back here."

"That's part of the fun," I say.

"If it's that much fun," Ma says, "then why aren't you sitting back here?"

"Ma, there's no steering wheel back there."

"How convenient."

So I let Ma drive and I sit in the back. Although Ma's a small woman, we discover within two blocks that all of her weight is in her foot.

We hear a siren. Ma says, "I wonder who they're after?"

"You're kidding, right, Ma?"

A cop pulls her over for speeding.

"You see, Officer," Ma tries to explain, "my son just bought this car and I had no idea how fast it was."

"Don't worry, Officer," I say, "she's grounded." The cop laughs . . . and gives her a ticket.

Dropping Ma off in front of the house. As she gets out of the car, she warns us, "Either of you mention this ticket to your father and you're in big trouble. Remember, I have plenty on both of you."

Danny and I both laugh as we pull away. The truth is, of course, she does.

Driving down the highway with The Fortune, Danny and me. The top's down and life's up.

There seem to be few moments in one's existence when the spirit allows itself to be totally filled with fun. We waste so much of our time worrying about being too young or too old. Too thin or too fat. Debating about whether or not to dump our lover or worried that they're debating about dumping us. Concerning ourselves with what other people think of us or with what we think of them. Upset because we can't handle our job or bored with our job or afraid that we're going to lose our job or angry because we've lost our job. Regretting the past and fearing the future. Worrying about dying. Worrying about living. But not today.

Danny and I lean our heads against the backs of the seats as the sun, waging war with the rushing wind, warms our faces as fast as the wind cools it. A delightful battle. The radio is on but we can't hear it. We choose, instead, to listen to the tune of the tires as they run along the road. If, indeed, there is a heaven, then moments like these are free samples.

About six months later, I am lying on the living-room floor watching television when Ma comes in from the kitchen. "Next week, Danny's going to be fifteen and a half," Ma tells me.

Still focusing all of my attention on the television. "Why are you telling me this? Do you want to give him a half-a-birthday party?"

"He's getting his driver's permit next week and you're the one who's going to teach him how."

"Why me?"

"I don't have the time," Ma says. "I'm doing a lot of your father's bookkeeping work now." Ma looks at me sympathetically. "Would you want to subject Danny to your father?"

Dad had tried to teach me how to drive. It wasn't pretty. We managed to survive each other for less than an hour. During the entire time, Dad alternately threatened to jump out of the car or push me out.

I actually learned to drive from Sammy Kackwater, who lived on the next block over. Sammy Kackwater was so unpopular that even though he owned his own car nobody wanted to hang around with him anyway. Basically, though, I found him to be a pretty nice guy. He did have those moments, however, when you wanted to cut his throat.

I started hanging around with Sammy a few months before I turned sixteen. One day, Sammy and I are riding around. I'm kidding him about his driving and Sammy replies, "If you think you can do any better, you're welcome to try."

He gets out of the car, walks around to the passenger side, and gets in while I slide behind the wheel.

Twenty minutes later, I'm driving sixty miles an hour on a four-lane highway. Sammy is a nice guy but not the world's brightest.

By my sixteenth birthday, I already know how to drive but I can't tell my parents that. After the hour in hell with my dad trying to teach me, we both come into the house shaking, me with fright and him with anger. Ma takes the keys out of Dad's hands and announces, "I'll teach him how to drive."

We get in the car and drive around the block a few times. Ma tells me to back up and turn around, which I do. She tells me to parallel park. I do that, too. She takes me out on some highways and we drive around for a few minutes. Then she has me drive us home.

Ma's nobody's fool. She obviously knows something's amiss but she says nothing.

When we walk back into the living room, Dad is still sitting on the couch shaking. Ma tosses him the car keys and says, "Now he knows how to drive. Honestly, you make such a big deal out of everything."

"I'll teach Danny," I say to Ma, "but I haven't got a lot of time right now myself. I'll have to make it a crash course."

Ma has already walked back to the kitchen but she hears me anyway. "Funny boy. Time to set the table, Donald. Be careful. Remember, last time you stabbed yourself with a fork."

A few days later, with me strangling my armrest, Danny inches The Fortune away from the house. The first time he puts his foot on the gas, he and the car jump together. But once he relaxes, Danny learns quickly. His only problem is that he tends to be too cautious.

"Danny," I warn him, "the way to avoid having problems behind the wheel is to do what's expected of you. Here we are on a main street," I say, "and you stop to allow someone from a side street to pull out in front of you."

"I'm just trying to be polite."

"But the person behind you," I point out, "almost rear ended you."

"Wouldn't they have been at fault?" asks Danny.

"That's not the point," I say. "Do what other drivers expect you to do and you cut down your chances of being involved in an accident.

"Let's say that you're on a highway and the speed limit is fifty-five. But everyone else is doing closer to sixty-five. Then you go with the flow. If you're approaching an intersection and the light changes to yellow, even though you may be able to slam on your brakes in time, it usually makes more sense to just go through the intersection. Do you understand what I'm saying?"

"Yes, I understand what you're saying," says Danny. "I should ignore all the laws and drive like a maniac."

"No," I say. "You have to drive more decisively, more confidently.

"I'm not telling you to be an aggressive driver. I'm saying, be more aggressive than you are. You're driving so cautiously you're driving scared and that's dangerous."

I discover that Danny is also a bit brain damaged when it comes to "right" and "left." He has to think about it. One afternoon, we're driving along. I say to him, "Turn right."

He turns left and almost broadsides an eighteen-wheeler.

"What the hell's wrong with you?" I scream. "I said right."

Danny meekly replies, "I thought you meant my other right."

A few days later, Danny and I go to a shopping mall. He wants to drive. As we are approaching an intersection, the light changes to yellow and Danny slams on the brakes to avoid going through the intersection. I'm not expecting it and he almost puts me through the windshield.

"What the hell did you do that for?"

"The light changed."

"To yellow," I say. "You had plenty of time to go through it."

"You drive a lot faster than I do," Danny explains.

"No, I don't," I say. "I drive with more confidence. If you're that afraid, you shouldn't be driving."

"Shut up." Danny is really starting to get upset.

"You're such a wimp!" I yell at him.

Danny pulls the car over to the curb, turns off the engine, gets out of the car, slams the door behind him, and begins walking down the street.

After waiting a few moments, I get behind the

wheel, restart the car, and drive along the curb as he
continues to walk down the sidewalk.

"Come, on, Danny, don't make such a big deal
out of it. If you don't get in this car right now, I'm
taking off. I'm serious, I've got to get to the mall. . . .
Come on, I was just kidding. . . . All right, I'm sorry
I called you a wimp."

Danny finally gets back in the car but he refuses
to drive. We are at the mall at least an hour before
things get back to normal.

On the way home, I drive. As we approach every
intersection with a light, I slow down or speed up to
catch a yellow light. Each time, I ask Danny what
he'd do, go through the intersection or brake? At
first, he really thinks about his answers. But after a
while, he just tells me what I want to hear.

In front of the house, when we're getting out of
the car, I say to him, "Danny, there's one thing I
can't teach you about driving—"

"I know, I know, I have to drive with more confidence."

"Well, hopefully, I can help you with that. But
the one thing I can't help you with is figuring out
how yellow lights know you're in a hurry."

Danny smiles but then adds, "The thing is, Donald, I'm not."

I am twenty and Danny's seventeen. New Year's Eve
Day. Tonight I'm taking a new girlfriend, Elaine
Pritzer, to a New Year's Eve party at the Palmer
House, one of Chicago's finer hotels. I figure that the
night is going to cost me about a week's salary. I've
even rented a tuxedo. Elaine's bought a new dress.
This could be the start of something big.

I don't care about the money because I'm having
my best day ever at the shoe store. But between han-

dling the high heels and running with the loafers, I'm trying to watch the weather as it develops outside the store window.

It is a typical midwestern late December day; about eighty thousand degrees below zero and there's a cold front moving in. The good news is that there is no snow. But around three o'clock, the good news starts evaporating.

At first, the flakes fall casually from the sky. When I close the store, however, at five o'clock, the snow is falling in a frenzy.

The bus ride home takes three times longer than usual. By the time I get in the house, I am already wondering if I'll be able to pick up Elaine on time.

Taking my snow-soaked shoes off at the door, throwing my coat into the guest closet. The television is on but no one is watching.

Yelling, "I'm home." We all do that when we come in the house—I have no idea why—unless we all come in together, of course.

Ma walks in from the kitchen. "You don't even wonder where your father is?"

"Ma, I just walked in. How would I know he's not home? Okay, Ma, where's Dad?"

"The truck broke down. He's stuck in a garage over on Seventy-eighth Street. He doesn't expect to get home much before nine."

"That's too bad." Even as I say the words, I'm bounding up the stairs two at a time. At the top, I see that the bathroom door's closed. "Hey, Danny, I've got to get in there. Got a big date tonight."

He yells back through the door. "Hey, so do I."

"You've had all day to get ready," I say. "I just got home from work."

"I worked today, too."

"Just hurry it up, all right?"

"All right, all right."

I go into the bedroom, flop down on the bed, and stare at the clock. About forty years later, Danny comes out of the bathroom. As I pass him in the hallway I say, "There better be some hot water left."

"There's plenty," he says, "but I ran out of toothpaste."

"I didn't even know you used it," saying the words as I close the bathroom door in order to shut off any attempt at verbal retaliation.

By the time I come out of the bathroom, Danny is already in his tuxedo. I had forgotten that he's going to a formal dance, too.

"Very snazzy," I say.

"Thanks." Danny heads downstairs.

Looking out the window as I struggle to put on my tuxedo. Now it is really snowing. Only speckles of night prevent the vision from being completely white.

A few minutes later, I go downstairs and into the kitchen.

Danny is just getting off the phone.

"Great," I say, "I've got to make a quick call." After telling Elaine that I'll be a few minutes late, I go into the living-room closet to get my topcoat.

Danny looks at me and says, "Your tie's on upside down."

"Your head's on upside down."

"I'm telling you," Danny says emphatically, "your tie's on wrong."

Looking in the mirror. He's right. "Help me with this thing, will you?"

Danny comes over, stands behind me, and unclips the tie. Then, after I have turned it right side up, he reclips it.

Ma comes into the living room. "Don't you two

boys look wonderful? You look so grown up." Danny and I mumble our thanks.

Ma says to me, "Now you know you have to drop Danny off at Angie's."

Turning on Danny. "You didn't tell me you needed a ride."

"I just found out two minutes ago," he says. "The guy we're doubling with, he hasn't gotten home from work yet because of the weather. But Angie's father said that if I could get to his house, he'd let me use his car."

"Where does she live?"

"Over near Tooley Park."

"That's in the exact opposite direction of where I'm going," I moan. "In this kind of weather, I'll never get there."

"Donald," Ma says sternly, "you are using the family car. In case you haven't noticed, Danny is a member of the family. You take him or you do not take the car."

"Look, Ma, I asked for the car at least a week ago," I say. "The moment I knew The Fortuno would be in the shop, and you said there'd be no problem."

"There is no problem," says Ma, "but you're taking Danny."

"I'm never going to get there on time—"

"You're just wasting time arguing about it," says Ma. "Now go."

All this time, Danny is just standing there listening to this. When you're the plaintiff, why bother saying anything when the judge is saying it for you? Then Danny looks at my midsection.

"Where's your cummerbund?"

"Damn it, I knew something was missing." Sprinting up the stairs. But when I check the hanger,

I find no cummerbund. The idiots at the rental place had forgotten it.

When I get back downstairs, Danny already has his topcoat on. "I don't have a cummerbund," I say to him. Looking at my watch again. "Maybe I'd better call Elaine and tell her—"

"That's just going to take more time," Ma says.

She's right. Throwing on my coat, not even bothering to button it. "You know, Danny, you're a pain in the ass. I've been planning this night for months and now you go and screw it up."

"Sorry. But it's not really my fault."

"When I was your age, I wasn't even going out on New Year's Eve." A lie, but who'd remember?

"Yes, you did," says Danny. "When you were seventeen, you went to a party over at Carl Chasing's house."

That answered that question. "Yeah," I respond, "but at least I went somewhere I could walk to."

"Dad drove you."

"But I could have walked," I say.

"If you weren't such a wimp."

"You want to start something?" I challenge.

"Right," says Danny. "We certainly are dressed for it."

"One more word, Donald," warns Ma, "and Danny will be taking the car and you will be walking."

"Fine, fine," I mumble as I put on my coat. "I should own a damn chauffeur's cap."

"After all the places your father and I have driven you."

Danny is wearing boots but I don't think I'll need any. If I have to, I'll just tiptoe to the car, that's all. Opening the front door. The entire front porch is obliterated by snow. Boots. Definitely boots.

After pulling them on, Danny and I push open the storm door and step out onto the porch. There is hardly a hint of angle where the steps are buried beneath. The wind is blowing fiercely, whipping the snow across my eyes. I can barely see the car, which is parked only a few dozen feet away.

Danny trudges silently behind me. I'm angry at him and he's angry at me for being angry at him.

Moving across the porch, my foot gingerly slips through the snow, searching for the first step. We basically slide down the stairs and are about halfway to the car when we hear Ma yelling from the door to us.

Fighting back through the storm all the way to the house. When we get near the door, Ma waves us back in. The shock of the house heat rattles my bones.

"Danny, Angie's father just called. He said it's simply too bad to be driving out there tonight but that you're more than welcome to come over and welcome in the New Year with Angie. He just doesn't want you and his daughter, and his car, on the road."

Danny looks at me and I glare back.

"No," he says, "I'm not going to bother. I can see Angie tomorrow when the weather lightens up."

Ma says, "Don't let Donald bully you. It's your New Year's Eve, too."

"No, really, it's okay," says Danny. He unbuttons his heavy coat, takes off his cummerbund, and hands it to me.

"Thanks, Danny." I fold it up and stuff it in my pocket. I want to get out of there before Danny changes his mind.

"Happy New Year, everybody," I say as I head back out the door. I don't wait for, nor do I hear, any replies. When I get to the car, I can't get the door open. At first I think it's locked. Then I realize that it's just frozen shut. Finally, I manage to pull it open.

Slipping the key into the ignition as the winter storm blusters around me. By now, the street looks barely passable. But I know that if I can get to a main street within the next few minutes, I'll still be all right. The plows might already be working them.

Turning the ignition, the engine whirls but doesn't turn over. Three more attempts get the same results. Now I'm afraid I'm going to flood it. I wonder if Danny had heard the car struggling to start. Unlike me, either Danny or Dad would have a fighting chance in a situation like this.

I sit in the car a few moments, waiting for the engine to recover from my attempts at starting it. Even I know that if I don't wait, I'll greatly increase the probability of flooding it.

Now, as I go to turn the ignition, through the maze of snow I see Danny standing at the front of the car. He signals for me to pop the hood so I do. He disappears behind the upraised hood for a moment and then yells to me, "Try it." I do and the engine roars into life.

Waving a thanks, I put the car into drive. Stuck. Danny walks to the back and, as I alternately put the car in drive and then neutral, he rocks it out of the rut and the car slides into the middle of the street.

Danny walks over to the driver's side. "It isn't packed down yet so just drive slowly and you should make it."

I roll the window down partially so he can hear me. "Look, I know it's asking a lot, but would you ride with me until I get to A hundred and eleventh Street, in case I get stuck?"

"Sure." He opens the back door and sits behind me. We drive in silence. Thinking about it, I decide to skip going to 111th Street and, instead, drive the six blocks straight to Kedzie Avenue. That way, I won't have to make any turns, a maneuver that might get me stuck in the ever-deepening snow. Danny, of course, realizes what I'm doing. I take his silence as consent.

But as we approach Kedzie Avenue, we can see that it's in even worse shape than the side streets. Two cars have already spun out and stalled, virtually blocking all traffic. There is no way for me even to get out on the street.

We pull into a closed gas station and stop under the canopy. The snow is only slightly less deep than it is everywhere else. There is a phone booth on the side of the station.

"I've got to call Elaine," I say. "She's expecting me."

I get out of the car, push my way through the snow storm, and somehow manage to fight my way past the folding doors of the phone booth.

The phone has barely rung when Elaine picks it up. She hardly waits to hear my voice. "Where are you?"

"I'm just a few blocks from my house—"

Elaine almost screams it. "Do you know what time it is?"

"It's snowing hard here and—"

"Come on," she says sarcastically, "there are a few flakes falling."

"A few flakes! There are accidents all over the place. Nothing's moving—"

Elaine interrupts, "The ground's hardly covered here. Just drive a few miles and you'll be out of it."

"I don't think you understand, Elaine. . . ."

"Fine," says Elaine flatly. "I'm going to call my girlfriend. Maybe I can catch a ride with her and her date before they leave."

"You're going to the dance without me?"

"Yes," says Elaine flatly. "I have to go," and she does.

Climbing back into the car. "What did Elaine say?" asks Danny.

"She was very understanding."

Slowly heading back home, we pass a few cars that have already been abandoned. It is now snowing even harder than it had been before. Reaching Trumbull Avenue, I have to make a left turn. But as the car dips into the corner, the wheels become trapped.

Danny gets out and tries to push, but the car won't budge. He gets back in the car, the front seat this time. His coat is speckled with snow from the spinning wheels.

"The weird thing," Danny says, "is it's New Year's Eve and we're the only ones out here."

It hadn't occurred to me but he's right.

"I guess," says Danny, "that people have either gotten where they're going or have decided not to go at all."

We are still five blocks from home. "We can't leave the car here," I say. "Maybe we can walk back and get some of the neighbors to help us."

"On New Year's Eve?" Danny asks.

"Good point."

An old man, walking his dog, offers to steer while we push. But after twenty minutes, we give up.

Sitting in the car, totally drenched from a mixture of melting snow and perspiration. The disk jockey on the radio announces that the old year only has ninety minutes left.

Feeling a hard bump on the car's back bumper, Danny and I turn around. Through the back window, in the shadow of the streetlight, we see the massive shoulders of Dad's potato chip truck.

Rolling down the window and looking behind me.

Only Dad's arm sticks out of the sliding door, waving forward, silently telling me he is going to push.

The potato chip truck delivers a few more hard bumps and some determined shoves before the car slides loose from the snow.

During the six-block ride back home, every time the car starts to stick, the potato chip truck bangs into its behind.

Ma is standing in the window when car and potato chip truck crawl up to the front of the house.

The three of us have hardly cracked open the front door when Ma begins firing. "I've been frantic with worry. Where have you all been? Danny, you didn't tell me you were going with Donald."

Then Ma starts aiming at me. "The moment you saw how bad it was out there, why didn't you just turn around and come home?"

Pointing at Dad, she says, "You said you'd be home by nine and it's nearly midnight."

"Midnight," Dad echoes. "It's almost the new year. Turn on the TV so we can get the countdown." Danny does and, a few seconds later, I'm kissing and hugging Ma and shaking hands with Dad and Danny. Not exactly the way I had planned on spending New Year's Eve but that's okay, too.

Dad's hungry. He hasn't had dinner yet. We all go into the kitchen. Dad makes sandwiches while Ma makes soup. Danny puts on the coffee and gets the pop ready. I set the table and help everybody else.

There is the usual scurrying-around-the-kitchen chatter. But when we sit down at our places, all conversation abruptly stops. Each of us, for our own reasons, silently savors the moment.

I have eaten thousands of meals at this table with these people. But now, for the first time, I realize that I will not eat thousands more. Remembering the words of Danny's essay. "There is a first time and a last time for everything."

Even now, the four of us rarely eat a meal together. Dad's putting in more time than ever. Ma has a part-time job at a neighborhood stationery store. I work five nights a week at the shoe store and Danny's always staying late at school for something.

Within a year, Danny will almost certainly go away to school. By then, maybe I'll have a better job and be able to afford my own apartment. Or maybe I'll start school at the junior college, get my grades up, and try and get into a good school or maybe . . . Beginnings are endings.

My parents never went out on New Year's Eve. I had always presumed they just didn't want to. My dad always referred to it as "Amateur Night" as if he were a professional partygoer or something.

For the first time and the last Ma talks about her father. In the early hours of that new year's birth, Ma tells Danny and me that her own father had died on New Year's Eve.

"He was fifty-five when I was born and my mother was nearly forty," Ma says. "They used to call me their homemade grandchild.

"When my father was in his seventies, I was just a teenager. Each morning, my mother would give him a dollar to spend at the tavern, the pool hall, or wherever old men go during the day. Sometimes," Ma laughs, "my mother wouldn't have a dollar so she'd just tell him she'd given him a dollar.

"One New Year's Eve, after dinner, Father said he was feeling quite ill. Mother wanted to call an ambulance but Father said he would just drive over to the hospital. Instead, Mother called a cab and the three of us went together.

"We dropped Father off at the emergency room

front door and then Mother and I went to the admissions office to take care of the paperwork. It was only a few minutes. By the time we got back to the emergency room, Father had passed away.

"I remember coming home at daybreak that morning, taking down the Christmas tree, putting away the ornaments, removing all the Christmas decorations from the house. So sad.

"Since then, I've always made it a point to go to bed before midnight on New Year's Eve."

"Until tonight," says Danny.

"Until tonight," repeats Ma.

Dad holds up his coffee cup. "Happy New Year."

Holding up our cups and glasses, we all return his salute.

After dinner, Ma and Dad go into the living room to watch an old movie on television. Danny and I clean up the dishes.

By the time we get into the living room, Ma and Dad have fallen asleep. The lights on the Christmas tree blink a kaleidoscope of colors throughout the room.

Looking out the window, Danny and I can see that the snow has finally stopped. The only white in the sky now is the twinkling dots of the distant stars.

"I'm still not tired," says Danny.

"Me neither."

"Want to take a walk?"

"Sure. Why not."

Both of us are still wearing our tuxedos but we decide not to bother changing. After all, they're rented. Putting on an avalanche of winter clothes, starting with the beanies and ending with the boots.

It takes a few shoves against a snowdrift just to get the storm door open wide enough to get outside.

Walking down the middle of the street, again remembering the words that Danny had written in his essay a few years earlier.

We truly are in a silent movie. The only sound comes from the efforts of our boots as they descend into the snow only to struggle out again in order to take the next step.

Waves of snow have crested over porches, windowsills, our car, and every other car on the street as well as up against the wall of the potato chip truck. White ribbons balance precariously on even the thinnest of branches.

The only scratch on the landscape, a set of tire tracks, has been almost completely erased by the falling snow that has followed it.

"It was strange, hearing Ma talk about her father," says Danny. "When you think about it, neither Ma nor Dad hardly ever talk about their parents."

"I wonder if we'll talk as rarely about them."

"It's hard for me to imagine Ma as a little kid," says Danny. "Obviously, at one time, she had to be. Just like everybody else, she started out as a baby, became a little kid, was even a teenage girl, like our age."

"That's weird."

"I know," says Danny. "I know. But I find it tough seeing Ma as an old lady, too. I know we're going to grow older, but for some reason I think Ma's going to be excused. She's just always going to be 'Ma.' "

We walk for a few minutes in silence. The only sign of life we see is a car crossing through an intersection a few blocks away.

"So how's Angie doing?" I ask. She's Danny's new girlfriend. He had met her at the restaurant where he's been working part time. "She's doing great. I really like her."

"You like them all."

"No, really. This girl, I mean, I really like her."

"You know, Danny, you seem to be very popular with the girls. It certainly can't be your looks."

"Thank you."

"And I'm more charming. How do you do it?"

Danny laughs. "I don't know. I'm nice to them. Sometimes I listen to their problems. Really, I just treat them like human beings."

"What a gimmick. I wouldn't have thought of that in a million years."

We walk a few more minutes in silence. Then Danny says to me, "My toes are beginning to go numb."

"Mine, too."

Up ahead, we see a stream of stores on a cross street.

"Is that Ninety-fifth Street?" I ask. "I can't believe we've walked that far."

"Sure is," says Danny. "We've gone a lot farther than I thought."

I remember that there's a twenty-four-hour coffee shop only a couple of blocks over. A few minutes later, Danny and I are huddling over steaming cups of coffee as we feel the heat of the shop melt the cold from our bones.

"So how's life in the shoe biz world?" Danny asks.

"Actually," I say, "although New Year's Eve day is usually quite slow, today was my best day ever."

"How so?"

"Two wedding parties and Cinderella came in," I say.

"Cinderella?"

"And two wedding parties," I repeat.

"That's a good day?" asks Danny.

"Wedding parties mean lots of shoes, at least three pairs," I say. "Besides, I find them fun."

"Why?"

"Because her wedding day is the most important day in this woman's life and she has to depend on the likes of me."

"Pathetic," agrees Danny.

"My sentiments exactly," I confirm. "Usually, the bride and her cohorts will come in and, after they've bought the shoes, she will give me this little swatch of cloth, usually about an inch square.

"She'll say to me, 'Now are you sure you can dye the shoes to match this color exactly? As you can see, it's not really empress pink or blossom pink or even baby bird pink . . . I guess it's closer to baby bird pink than anything . . .'

" 'Don't worry,'' I'll assure her. 'We can match it.'

" 'You've got to promise me you'll match it exactly. Promise me, now promise me.'

" 'I promise, I promise.' I'll tell her, 'Madam, we have a chemist, full time, on the staff. He will spend hours, days, weeks if necessary, mixing and matching colors until he comes up with the perfect combination for you.'

"By the time they get to their cars, I will have gone into the back of the store, looked up pink on the chart, got out the old paint roller, and knocked off those shoes.

"She and her wedding party will come back about three weeks later. Let's say that the shoes have turned out—oh—black. Usually, there's a lot of weeping and wailing . . . life-threatening gestures.

"Being the professional shoe salesman that I am,

I go with one of two stock replies: 'Different cloths take colors differently,' or 'Yes, miss, I have to agree that these shoes do look black. But you have to realize that it's because of the lights in here. When you get these shoes under the proper lights,' whatever the hell that is, 'they'll look just fine.'

"If things really get nasty, you can always say, 'Miss, instead of these shoes, what I'd be worried about if I were you is, when the person performing the ceremony says, "Will you have this woman . . ." and half the congregation stands up and says they already have.' "

"I want to hear about Cinderella," says Danny.

"She was an ugly machine, had the personality of a thornbush, and not a brain in her head, but she was definitely my Cinderella. You see, I sold her the 'Galaxy' shoes."

"All right, I'll bite," says Danny. "What are the 'Galaxy' shoes?"

"We have a system in the store," I explain. "When a pair of shoes doesn't sell in a certain amount of time, the manager puts a star on the box, which means you get another fifty cents if you sell them. The longer the pair of shoes is around, the more stars it gets. We have one pair of shoes where the box is nothing but stars, hence the name 'Galaxy' shoes.

"Two months ago, all of us salesmen kicked in ten bucks apiece as an added incentive for someone to sell those 'Galaxy' shoes."

Smiling up at the ceiling. "And I am that someone."

"What do they look like?" Danny asks.

"I don't even want to think about it. They're so ugly, a dead nun wouldn't be caught dead in them. They're mostly black—they have red on them somewhere—I think they have cleats . . . eye hooks; they definitely have eye hooks and they lace up beyond the knees. Did I mention the fog horn? And I'm sparing you the more gruesome details.''

"How much did you make?''

"At least ninety bucks.''

Danny is impressed. "That's a lot of money for selling a pair of shoes.''

"Not 'a' pair of shoes, 'the' pair of shoes. I say to her, 'Lady, these are million-dollar shoes.' Of course, I don't mention who's getting the million.

"What I can't understand,'' I say, "is how women can spend so much time shopping.''

"I like to shop,'' says Danny.

"This would come as a shock to most women,'' I say, "but men think shopping is where you go out, you buy something, and you go home. And men always buy things for women that make no sense to a man. Flowers . . . jewelry . . .''

Danny says, "I like flowers and jewelry.''

I ignore his comment. "But does a woman ever buy a man what a man really wants? Another woman? Nah.

"For women,'' I continue, "shopping is a religious ritual. They know all the little tricks. Last week, just before Christmas, this couple is standing in front of the store. The guy says to her, 'Why can't you just buy the shoes now and we can get home that much sooner?'

"She says, 'Because we drove here.'

" 'So?' the guy says.

"She says, 'Well, now, I have to walk around awhile until my feet swell to their normal size and then I buy the shoes.'

"She says to him, 'I thought you had some things you had to get.''

"He says, 'Well, I was going to buy some underwear.' ''

Walking back home. During the time we've spent in the coffee shop, the sanctity of the fallen snow has been repeatedly vilified by the awakening world. It's still dark but it won't be for much longer. Snowplows are clearing the main roads while numerous tire tracks have sliced open the side streets.

All over the city, the air is seeping out of the New Year's Eve balloons, including ours.

Walking home, following the ruts in the road.

"It's your turn to shovel the sidewalk."

"No, it isn't. It's yours."

"You're crazy. I did it last time."

"You can't count the last time. You swept the sidewalk off with a broom."

"Still counts."

"Does not."

"Does so."

"Does . . ."

12

No matter how old Danny and I get, Ma still comes up here in the middle of the night and goes through the motions of tucking us in.

One night, it must have been at least three in the morning, I am sitting up in bed worrying. Danny is sleeping like a rock. That afternoon, he had received a full scholarship to one of the best universities in the country. I don't begrudge him that. God knows he's earned it. But I've already been at the shoe store two years and I'm afraid I'm going to spend my whole life there.

That's what Ma and I get to talking about. She asks me what I want to be. I don't even mention the possibility of playing the outfield. I do tell her that I'm thinking about being a writer. Exactly what kind of writer, I'm not sure. But I tell Ma, ''I know I need more education and, besides, you can starve to death trying to do something like that.''

Ma tells me I should do what I love and the money will take care of itself. ''Donald,'' she says, ''never walk a road that doesn't lead to your heart.'' Then she tucks me in.

I am twenty-one and Danny's eighteen. Exactly. His birthday lands on a Friday this year but everybody in the family has to work on Friday night so we put off the birthday party bash until Saturday night. As Dad points out, somewhere in the world, it must still be Friday. Yeah, Dad.

Right after dessert, Ma, Dad, and I present Danny with the only gift he's been mentioning for almost every day during the past six weeks, a camera.

Danny goes berserk. I've never seen him so excited. He starts taking pictures of everything: us, Blackie, the rooms of the house, furniture, until he runs out of film.

He goes out and buys more. While he's gone, his girlfriend, Angie, comes over. She had to work late. As soon as he walks in, Danny begins taking pictures of her. Then he asks me to take pictures of him and Angie.

While all this is going on, Danny is constantly blubbering about how he wants to be a professional photographer. I'm not too thrilled by the thought since, even with my eyes closed, I'm still seeing pops of yellow.

I am twenty-one and Danny's eighteen, a week, and a day. After dinner, I'm hurrying to get out of the house because I'm meeting some of my buddies at the LaTours Club, which is the only bar in the neighborhood that caters to people who are still living within the shadows of their twenty-first birthday.

Already I'm running late because I'd had to clean up the supper dishes. That goofy scissors, paper, rock game. Now even Ma is beating me at it.

When I get up here, to the bedroom, to change clothes, Danny's doing likewise, getting ready for a date with Angie.

"Too bad we're not closer in age," I tell Danny.

"Why?"

"Because we could go to the LaTours Club together. It would be fun."

"When I'm twenty-one, we can go together then," says Danny.

"No, it'll be too late for me. No one over twenty-three ever goes to the LaTours."

"Why not?"

"I don't know. They just don't." I sit down on the edge of my bed. "There are certain things you need to know about LaTours before you start going there if you don't want to look like a jerk."

Danny is rummaging through a drawer. "Are we out of socks?"

"No, there's some downstairs in the laundry basket. Look, do you want to hear this stuff about LaTours or not?"

Danny's now searching under the bed for a missing shoe. "Donald, it'll be three years before I can even go there."

He peeks over the top of the bed at me and can see that it's important to me that I impart this knowledge to him. Danny sits up on top of his bed. "Okay, tell me about LaTours."

"First of all," I say, "the only night that anybody goes to the LaTours Club is Friday night. No reason. That's just the way it is. No one is even sure the building is there any other night of the week.

"There's a dance floor but no one dances until

at least midnight. Instead, you stand around and talk.''

Danny slides his butt to the edge of the bed. He's anxious to get this over with. "Anything else?"

"Yes. Although the place will be filled with guys you grew up with, you never discuss anything you did together as 'kids,' that is, any activity that goes back more than six weeks."

Danny stands up.

"One more thing. No one is allowed to drive home drunk. The reasoning is simple. Since we all live within a couple miles of LaTours, if a drunk kills somebody on the way home, it's most likely going to be one of us."

"Makes sense to me," says Danny. "Could I bring Angie there?"

Now I stand up. "No. The whole idea of going to LaTours is to meet somebody. God, sometimes you can be so dense."

"I already have somebody," says Danny.

"Yeah, like you're going to know her in three years."

"I think so," says Danny. "I told you I really like Angie."

"Three years. Most people don't even keep a car three years."

I walk over to the closet and begin looking for a light jacket. Danny says to me, "Take the brown one."

"But that's your favorite jacket. It's brand new."

"So what?"

"But I'm just going to a bar. I can wear one of the others. Besides, you know what slobs my friends are. Somebody might spill something on it."

Danny says, "You like it, take it. It's just a jacket."

So I do. But just to make sure nothing happens to it when I go into LaTours, I leave it in the car.

I mean, it was no big deal, Danny lending me that jacket. Yeah, it was a big deal.

I come in late that night from the La Tours Club. Danny's sitting on the bed, jumping up and down as high as he can get. He says to me, "Tonight, Angie and I decided that we're going to get married."

"Not tomorrow," I say. "I have a softball game."

"I'm serious," says Danny. "She's wonderful . . . she's gorgeous . . ."

When a guy says that a woman is wonderful and gorgeous, rather than the other way around, you know he's serious.

Danny says, "I don't know exactly when I'm going to marry her, but I'm going to marry her, you can be sure of that . . . and you can be my best man."

"You're just saying that because you know Ma would make you anyway."

Danny laughs. Then he says, in a bad imitation of Ma, " 'Remember, your friends come and go but you only have one brother.' Nah, I'd choose you anyway."

As Danny begins to talk about Angie again, another burst of energy pops out of him. "Angie and I are going to have lots of kids. Then you can get married and have lots of kids and we'll live right near each other and our kids can hang around with each other just like we did. I mean, you and I will still hang around with each other after we have our own families, you know, but it'll be different then, you know."

Then Danny says, "I wonder what we'll be like when we're in our forties?"

He lives another ten hours.

13

The next day, a Saturday morning. Dad's working all day and Ma has gone to visit one of her sisters-in-law so she won't be home until late afternoon either.

When I get up that morning, I can see that it's going to be a sunny, warm day. I decide to call the store manager and ask him if I can have the day off. He says that it'll be no problem as I presumed he would. It's a very slow time of the year for the shoe business.

I then call Nancy, a girl I had met a couple of weeks earlier. We have a date for this evening. I ask her if she wants to get together in the late afternoon so we can take a boat ride on Lake Michigan and then have dinner somewhere downtown. She loves the idea.

Just as I'm getting off the phone, Danny walks

into the kitchen. This summer, he's working as an assistant manager at the restaurant. He's wearing his uniform, which consists of a white shirt with the restaurant's logo, a blue tie with the restaurant's logo, and black slacks. He asks, "What are you doing home?"

"I'm taking the day off," I say. "Today, I'm going to be a bum."

"So what makes this day different than any other?"

"You're a funny guy, did you know that, Danny? Very funny guy."

Danny sits down at the kitchen table with a cup of coffee while I'm going through the cabinet shelves looking for a box of cereal that actually has some cereal.

"What time are you going on your date?" asks Danny.

"Why?" I ask suspiciously.

"Because," Danny explains, "I'm getting home early from work today. I thought, maybe, I could take The Fortune to work."

Danny's job is only about fifteen minutes away by car but thirty-five minutes by bus and nearly an hour's walk. But Danny loves to walk so if the weather's decent that's what he usually does.

"Sorry," I say, "I just made plans to go out late this afternoon."

"That new girl, Nancy?"

"Yep."

"What time this afternoon?" Danny asks.

"What time are you getting home from work?"

"Come on," Danny says.

"I'm leaving around four-thirty," I say.

"Terrific, I'll be home by four."

"Did I say four-thirty? I meant three-thirty."

"Don't be such an ass," Danny says.

"Ah, you sure are a smoothie when it comes to talking people out of their cars."

"Forget it," says Danny.

"Are you sure you'll be home by four o'clock?"

"Absolutely."

"The keys are on the counter. The tank's full so don't even bother stopping for gas." God, but I was feeling magnanimous.

"All right!" Danny jumps up from his chair. "Thanks a lot, Donald, I mean, really, thanks."

"Sure," I say. "You plan on putting the top down?"

"Yeah," says Danny apprehensively.

"The left latch is sticking a little. You might want to watch it."

"Yeah, sure," Danny says. He grabs the keys, zips out of the kitchen, and two seconds later I hear him bounding up the stairs.

After finishing my cereal, I go into the living room, drop down on the couch, and begin reading the newspaper. A moment later, Danny comes down the stairs.

"Thanks again for letting me use The Fortune."

"Sure. By the way, did you remember to make your bed?" At that time, Ma had a thing about unmade beds.

"Oh, damn. Can you do it for me?" Danny asks.

"Ah . . ."

"I'd do it for you."

"Yeah . . . yeah."

"Thanks." Danny walks out the door.

That was it.

Around one o'clock, a policeman comes to the door.

He asks me who I am and I tell him. He asks me

if I have a brother named Daniel. Then, somehow, I know it's over.

For three hours, I sit on the front porch, waiting for Ma and Dad to come home.

Remembering a late-night conversation that Danny and I had a few weeks earlier. He had just spent hours studying for a science test. Now we were lying in our beds waiting for sleep.

"Think about it," says Danny. "Light travels at about one-hundred eighty-six thousand miles a second. So if you traveled a billion years at the speed of light, where could you possibly be?"

"Iowa?"

"Funny. It's so weird," says Danny, awed by his own thoughts. "Since light images are always traveling outward from the earth . . . if there was a telescope powerful enough and far enough away . . . you could look back on earth and see the age of the dinosaurs.

"Just think, if you sit on the front porch tomorrow, somewhere, out in space, billions of years from now, someone will be able to see you."

Wondering now if Danny could see me.

One-hundred eighty-six thousand miles a second. Compared to death, light is a crawler. I had been with Danny only a couple of hours earlier but now he couldn't be farther away than if he had left a billion years ago at the speed of light.

Ma and Dad. I could contact them right now if I wanted to, but what would be the point? Let them have these last few hours.

Agonizing over the "if onlys" that would have kept Danny from being at that intersection at that precise moment. If only Danny had taken the time to make his bed. If only we had argued about it more. If only the car keys had been upstairs on the dresser.

If only he had needed to stop for gas. If only he had eaten a bigger breakfast or a smaller one. If only the coffee hadn't been ready. If only I had not taken the day off. If only my boss had said no. If only Nancy had said no. If only I had said no. If only the day had not been so beautiful . . . I would not be sitting on this porch.

Realizing. I have never gone more than a couple of days without seeing Danny. Now I will go a lifetime.

I will not be best man at his wedding nor will he be at mine. Our children will not play with each other. There will be no "Uncle Danny."

When I need to talk—to someone who's more than a friend . . . more than a relative—there will be no one.

We will not challenge each other to middle-aged games of basketball on driveways in suburbs that have yet to be built and laugh at each other and ourselves as we struggle to catch our breaths.

We will not tease each other about the bald spots and the expanding waistlines.

We will not see each other's new cars, or new apartments or new homes or new wives. I will not call him to tell him I got the new job, that I've met someone special . . . I'm engaged . . . I'm married . . . I'm a father . . . I'm divorced . . . I've been fired . . . I've met someone special.

I will not call him up and tease him when he turns thirty or forty or fifty. When I begin new decades, he will not call me.

I will not attend his children's graduations or their weddings. I will not be able to brag to him about my kids or be proud of his.

We will not meet in some restaurant for a quick cup of coffee, just to talk.

We will not help each other when Ma and Dad get old. We will not console each other when they die.

We will not get together just to get together because brothers like to do that.

We will not sit at kitchen tables or on front porches or park benches and wonder where the years have gone.

I think about yellow lights. Sitting on the porch that afternoon, I keep asking myself, had he gone through a yellow light and now that's why he was where he was? Or worse, was he indecisive going through the intersection because of all the things I had said to him? Or worse . . . Realizing that all of these thoughts now don't matter at all.

How do yellow lights know when you're in a hurry?

The strange thing is, the longer I sit on the front porch, the madder I get at Danny. How could he have been so careless? How could he have been so stupid? How could he do this to us?

Ma and Dad pull up together. He had picked her up from my aunt's house. Dad's in a great mood. Everything has gone perfectly for him today. Ma's in a good mood, too. I tell them.

I remember exactly what I said and how they reacted. But there's no point in repeating it. You know these kinds of things can happen and there's a small part of you that constantly worries that it will. Then, suddenly, the worrying's over.

That night, the neighbors come over and sit in the living room, devastated by what has happened to us. On the way home, they are exhausted with relief that it hasn't happened to them. Human nature.

The announcer on television says, ''It's ten-thirty, curfew time. Do you know where your children are?''

Dad sits up all night in his easy chair. He says, "Danny's never stayed out all night and I've never gone to sleep until he's come home."

It is shortly after midnight when I leave the house. The day is finally over. Walking through a night that is darker than I have ever seen.

If Danny had to go, I ask myself, wouldn't a long illness have been better? I would have had time to say all the things to him that I want to say now. I would have had time for the anger, for the sorrow, for the acceptance.

Remembering when we were kids at the park swimming pool, the water brutally cold. I would start out with just the big toe. Danny would dive right in.

Better for me, not for Danny.

I recall Danny talking about death a couple of years ago. An elderly neighbor had died. Late at night, Danny and I are walking home from a friend's house. We are both in a silly mood.

Danny says, "The thing that bothers me about dying is that it's so embarrassing."

"Embarrassing?"

"Yeah," he says, "There you are, living your life, having a great time, doing what you want to do, working, playing, goofing around, whatever, and, all of a sudden, six people have to carry you everywhere you go. It's just so embarrassing."

Embarrassing. Thinking of a football game I'd watched last year. The halfback runs up the middle and gains twelve yards. A teammate helps him up. Two others pat him on the back as he rejoins the huddle. On the next play, the halfback jumps up for a pass and a defensive lineman knocks his legs out from under him.

The halfback crumples to the ground holding his knee. He's in great pain. For a moment, a few of his teammates step toward him and stare. But they instinctively know that if they look too long, they'll see themselves. They are embarrassed by their own frailty. While attendants and assistant coaches gather around him, his teammates return to the huddle. He is no longer one of them. The game is for those who can play it.

Dreading what's coming in the next few days. Seeing them, all of them, hearing the trite expressions I've said, too. "If there's anything I can do . . ."

Six months ago, the father of another salesman at the shoe store dies of cancer. When I hear about it, that's what I say to him, "If there's anything I can do . . ."

His anger and frustration reply, "Well, if you're God, and you've been keeping it a secret, there is one favor I'd like to ask of you."

Almost certainly, someone is going to say to me, "Time heals all wounds." Perhaps. But then, time creates all wounds, too.

Losing Danny, a high price for turning twenty-one. Remembering Ma's words, "Losing is as much a part of life as breathing. Losing, and learning to go on and live again, is the only kind of winning that truly matters."

Walking so quickly that I am almost running. Perspiration pours down my face. Staying off the main streets and away from the lights. Before I realize it, I have walked out of my neighborhood and into another. Only occasionally does one of the darkened houses contain a pail of light. Looking at my watch. Already 2:00 A.M.

Time. A few months ago, Danny and I are lying in our beds, waiting for sleep, and he asks me to do him a favor the next day. Now I don't even remember what it was. I tell him I'd like to but I don't have the time. That's all he has to hear.

"You don't have the time?" he says. "You're alive, aren't you? So you do have time."

"Look," I say, "I'm tired. I don't want to start a long discussion on this . . ." But it's already too late.

"Time. Such a strange commodity," says Danny. "A lifetime can seem like a moment. A moment can seem like a lifetime.

"People talk about 'saving' time. Ridiculous. How can you 'save' time when you're spending time to do it?

" 'He's living on borrowed time.' Where could you possibly 'borrow' time and what would you pay for interest?

" 'Where does the time go?' That's an interesting one," says Danny. "Where does the time go?

" 'Time is money.' But I've never heard of a rich man on his death bed saying, 'Here's a million, give me another hour.'

"People say, 'You know, when my time comes,' when what they are really referring to is when it no longer comes."

Dying at eighteen. At nine, Danny was middle-aged.

Eighteen. The average eighteen-year-old male consumes over forty-five hundred calories a day.

Eighteen. Richard Rodgers was eighteen when he wrote "Manhattan."

Eighteen. The odds of surviving your eighteenth year are approximately two thousand to one.

Eighteen. The average eighteen-year-old will live to seventy-eight.

Eighteen. If you're a fly, that's an eternity. If you're a redwood, you're hardly a seedling. If you're Danny, it's a lifetime.

Finally, I turn around and slowly begin walking back toward home.

Thinking. Danny wasn't a famous actor or a famous politician or a famous anything. His death will not be mentioned on the front pages of the newspapers. The anchors on the evening news won't talk about his achievements. But most of those to whom we give such honors were less than he. The meek may inherit the earth, but they certainly do leave it quietly.

The first day without Danny. The phone rings very early. Dad answers it. He listens for a few moments, says "Yes," once or twice and then hangs up.

He looks at me. "Get some nice clothes for your brother."

For an instant, I don't understand. Then I do. Going upstairs to the bedroom, opening the closet, and grabbing the items of clothing quickly. I do not want to think about what I am doing. I grab a sport coat and then put it back, taking the brown jacket instead.

Throughout the morning, the phone and the doorbell constantly ring but no one really talks. Food is brought but no one eats. My mind is filled with a million thoughts but I refuse to think.

In the early afternoon, I get a call from the body and fender shop where The Fortune's been towed. Insurance forms, papers to sign, all of that.

I don't want to drive anywhere so I call Warren Marker, who's home from college, and he drives me over.

Warren waits in the car while I go in to take care of things. Behind the small office and garage that borders the street is a massive yard, rimmed by a sheet metal fence topped by barbed wire.

As the man walks me through the yard, we are surrounded by crushed hunks of steel that once were cars. One has been so smothered that its steering wheel is smashed against its roof.

I being to wonder just how badly The Fortune has been damaged when I am suddenly standing in front of it.

The left rear tire is flat. There's a big dent in the driver's door. The windshield is slightly cracked. Whoever put the top up couldn't hook the left latch. That's it. I realize now that I have been hoping that The Fortune had been mutilated beyond recognition.

Driving home with Warren, I ask him to do me a favor and he agrees. Six weeks later, I receive a check from a used-car lot.

When Warren drops me off in front of the house, Dad is sitting on the front porch. Sitting down beside him. Dad tells me that the police officer who was at the scene of the accident is a relative of one of the neighbors from the next block. The officer had stopped by a few minutes earlier to tell Dad what he knew, which wasn't much.

A simple accident, the kind that happens thousands of times, every day, all over the world. Two cars, traveling at moderate speed, if that, hit at an intersection. No one knows, or will ever know, which car got there late or which one got there early. The other driver, a seventy-year-old man, suffered a cut lip and a bloody nose. Danny's neck simply snapped in the wrong direction.

A minor accident in every way except one.

Dad cries.

For something to do, I read the newspaper. The obituary page. I do not think about looking for it. I simply do. The name is there. I have no idea who called or gave the information. Nor do I see the purpose in it all.

I tell myself that after all this is over, I will make

out a will. No wake. No funeral. No anything. Just get me out of the way. To this day, I have yet to do it.

Both nights the wake is packed. The young always draw well. Every now and then, someone in the back of the room chuckles over something. What else can you do? But to this day, Ma remembers every one of them and has never forgiven them.

Not fair. I know that all of this, for all of them, in just a few weeks will be nothing more than an unpleasant memory. In a few years a bookmark used to place other events in their lives. "Marge, when did I buy the yellow Buick? . . . Yeah, that's right. The same summer that Danny Cooper kid died."

I remember only one thing about the funeral. Our church has a choir loft that you can barely see from the main floor. As the procession is moving out of the church, a trumpet begins playing . . . very loudly . . . very badly . . . "Oh, Danny Boy."

A couple of days after the funeral, I walk into the drug store, which is about a block from the house, to buy a candy bar or something. The woman behind the counter is Mrs. Seldman, a neighbor. She says, "Your brother was in last week and left a roll of film to be developed." She holds up a small rectangular envelope. "They came in this morning. Do you want to take them?"

She knows, of course. Everyone knows.

I debate a moment. "Yeah, sure, of course."

She hands the envelope to me. I don't think to pay for them. She doesn't ask.

Walking down the street, squeezing the envelope too tightly in my fist, feeling the photos bow from the pressure. Reliving the moments that are now preserved in this envelope. There is a wastebasket up ahead. I walk past it to the mailbox on the corner.

Opening it and tossing in the envelope. Now there's no temptation to retrieve it.

The first year is drenched in melancholy. Refusing to look into the valleys. Refusing to look up at the mountains for fear I'll never see the plains again.

Sporadic and spontaneous outbursts of joy, which the human spirit instinctively ignites to salvage its sanity, are quickly doused by the cold dreary splash of reality.

Angie is there for everything. But she is just a girlfriend. Nothing more. I know that within a few months—a year at most—her wound will heal. Perhaps a scar will remain but, after all, anyone who's been on this earth awhile has plenty of those.

But I am wrong. On the first anniversary of his death, Ma tells me that she and Dad found a rose on his grave. She wonders who could have left it. I wonder who else it could possibly be.

But I presume that the gesture will end soon enough. There'll be new boyfriends, new lovers, a new husband.

But it doesn't end. Every year, to this day, a rose appears.

I hear that she does not marry until she's thirty-six, eighteen years after Danny. The marriage is over in less than ten months. I have no idea who she married but I feel sorry for him anyway. Tough to compete against someone who will always be perfect. Who will always be young.

I lose him when I am twenty-one and he is eighteen. At thirty-six, I realize that I have lived two of his lifetimes.

At thirty-nine, I have now lived as long without a brother as I have lived with one.

At forty-one, it's been twenty years.

At forty-two, I have lived another lifetime since I've lost him.

At forty-six, twenty-five years.

Three months after his death, I turn twenty-two. Danny has never missed a family birthday party. Now he will never attend another one. Nor will any of us. No party. Just a cake.

14

Now, somehow knowing that it's there, I get down on one knee to look under the lone bed. The brown box. Gently picking it up and holding it in my hands.

After Danny, I never spend another night in this room. Usually, I just sleep on the couch or on the living room floor.

A couple of weeks later, Dad has me throw out Danny's bed. I have to drag it down the stairs, through the yard, and out into the alley.

Ma wants to keep everything. Dad wants to throw out everything. Gradually, Dad wins. Now, it's down to just this one box.

I've never looked but Ma's told me what's inside anyway: Danny's glasses. His wallet, keys, his favorite paperback, the mouthpiece from his trumpet, school papers, some of them going all the way back to the eighth grade. Ma saves that sort of stuff.

I take the box, walk down the stairs and back out onto the front porch again. Sitting down on the top step. Savoring the fall sun as it heats my face.

After Danny, no more big dinners. We'd order a pizza or go out and get hot dogs or hamburgers. Sometimes, each of us would just make something for ourselves. Holidays, we'd go to a restaurant.

Sometimes, when no one was home, I'd go through the house and shout his name. I don't know why. Sometimes when I called home, I'd pray that he'd answer the phone and, if he did, I'd act as if nothing at all had ever happened. Sometimes Ma or Dad would say, "Would one of you boys . . ." Then they'd correct themselves.

Now there's no man on this earth I can truly call "brother."

15

Realizing that the phone has been ringing. Feeling as if I weigh a million pounds, I brace my hands against my knees and use the railing to push myself up. Walking through the living room, my legs moving with the indifferent rhythm of resignation.

Picking up the phone, I begin to say "Hello," but Ma doesn't even wait for it.

"Where were you?"

"I was sitting on the front porch."

"It took you all that time to come in from the front porch?"

"I'm very tired, Ma, very tired."

"Did you find the brown box?"

"I found the box."

"Are you sure it's the right one?" Ma asks.

Even I am startled as I hear my voice explode in anger. "I said I've got the damn box."

"There's no need for you to swear or to use that tone of voice," Ma says.

"Maybe there's no need for you, but sometimes I need to swear."

"I certainly don't have to hear that kind of language."

"I don't care if you don't have to hear it—" Forcing my voice to calm itself down. "I've got the box."

"With you right now?" Ma asks.

"No, it's on the front porch."

Now Ma becomes upset. "Dear God, you didn't leave it out there? Go get it. Someone could steal it. I can't believe you would—"

"Nobody's going to steal the damn thing. Even if they did, what's the difference? Would the world end?"

Ma almost whispers it. "A large part of mine would."

My voice, struggling to control its passion, drops each word deliberately. "Ma, it's just a box with things in it. That's all."

Ma's voice grows heavy in anger. "I don't tell you how to live your life—"

"That's not exactly true—"

"I don't tell you where to live or what to do. You'll never know how many times in the past twenty years I wanted you to come home. But did I ever nag you?"

"Ma, I'm here now."

Her voice curdles into anger. "While we're talking, someone could be taking that box. What is wrong with you?"

"All right, all right, all right, I'll get the damn box."

I pound the phone down on the counter, rush

through the living room, and throw open the storm door. Grabbing the brown box off the front porch, I walk back past the door while it is still wide open from my assault of a split second earlier.

Picking up the receiver as I slam the brown box down on the kitchen table. Almost screaming. "Now I've got the damn box, all right? I'm looking right at it. I'm touching it, okay?"

Ma's voice now carries that bland and controlled tone of righteous reason. "Can you look inside to make sure the wallet's there? . . ."

I am screaming now. "No, I'm not going to look inside."

"I just want you to check for—"

"I'm not going to check for anything."

Ma persists. "If you could just—"

I'm out of control now. "No, no, no."

She begins to plead.

"How can you be so insensitive to my feelings? How can you not care about—"

"I don't care?" I hear myself shouting. Grabbing the reins and feeling my words fight back as they strain to run wildly away from me.

"I came to this house, didn't I? I searched every room for this brown box, didn't I? I even went to the upstairs bedroom, and I told you I didn't want to do that. And you tell me I don't care about your feelings? I've got to go."

Ma persists. "You don't care about my feelings—"

The strength goes out of my voice. "Yeah," I counter, "as if you cared about mine. I've got to go."

"Donald—"

Screaming it. "I've got to go!"

Hanging up the phone. Angry, exhausted, and already beginning to feel real crummy about the whole thing.

Knowing that I've got to get out of this house
right now. Grabbing the brown box off the table. Almost running back through the living room and out
the front door, slamming the heavy one behind me
so that it locks automatically. But by the time I reach
the last step of the porch, I feel my emotions gasping
to catch their breath. My body sits as my emotions
collapse.

Placing the brown box next to me.

Talking to Ma that way. No point, no point in
that at all. Me and Ma . . . we're too much alike.

That autumn—God, it all seems so long ago—that
autumn . . . I start college at one of the best universities in the country. "Cooper, D." "Daniel,"
"Donald," they never notice the difference.

Time to grow up. Four tough years. Before college, I'd always thought of myself as a smart-ass and
a dreamer. Now I make my living as a comedy writer.
A smart-ass's dream come true.

Three summers later, Dad has a heart attack sitting in his easy chair. Usually, he'd fall asleep and
then, around one or two in the morning, he'd wake
up and go to bed for a couple of hours.

Ma hears him from the bedroom. She calls an ambulance and they rush him to the hospital. Then Ma
calls me where I'm staying at college. I always
worked and took courses during the summer.

It takes me over eight hours to drive in from
school. By the time I get to the hospital, Dad has
survived the critical phase and is now in the intensive care unit. Meeting Ma in the hallway.

"How's he doing?"

"He's conscious," Ma says, "but he's sleeping
most of the time. The doctors said they don't know
how much damage has been done." Ma pauses. "The
next few days are critical. He's allowed only one vis-

itor for ten minutes every two hours. It's almost time now. Why don't you go in and see him?''

Walking into the intensive care room. It is dimly lit. The only sounds are the beeps of the blips as they scurry across their screens and the even breathing of the machines interlaced with the labored breathing of the patients.

Walking by the beds of other patients, their bodies trapped by a tangle of tubes and wires. Marionettes at rest.

Finding Dad's bed, I look down at him. Fifty-four. Not ancient but certainly on the first pages of growing old. His eyes flutter open. I pat his hand. "You're doing fine, Dad, just fine." A few moments later, his eyes close. He gives no indication that he has heard or understood me.

I want to say something but what? If I say what my soul tells me, it'll sound like I'm saying good-bye. I want to say, "I love you, Dad." But I convince myself that if my life hasn't already told him, there's no point in saying it now. I feel my spirit shriveling up in sadness.

Sitting down next to Ma in the waiting room. "How does he look?" Ma asks.

"He looks good."

"Does he really?" Ma wants to be assured again.

"Yes. He looks good. He really does."

I'm lying, of course. How do you look good in an intensive care unit?

If Dad was "looking good" he'd be jumping on and off his truck as he delivered his potato chips.

Looking good is caressing the flowers you planted last fall.

Looking good is making a diving catch in center field and then throwing the runner out at the plate.

Looking good is playing a trumpet so sweetly that tears well up in the eyes of the ears that hear it.

Ma doesn't ask but I say it again anyway. "Yeah, he looks good."

About ten days later, Dad's moved to a regular hospital room. I'm in the middle of some final exams so he's there a few days before I get to see him.

We are sitting there talking when the nurse brings in his dinner.

"What's the soup tonight?" he asks.

"Split pea."

"Oh, boy," Dad says excitedly, "terrific. That's my favorite. I just love split pea soup."

The nurse looks at me and says, "Every night, it's a different soup and every night, it's his favorite. I tell you, the man never disappoints me."

About two weeks later, while he was still in the hospital, Dad had another heart attack and passed away.

The last time I was in this house was the day of Dad's funeral. I handled that pretty well. You expect to lose your father. But I told Ma I couldn't come home again. Everything in this house, everything in this neighborhood, reminded me of Danny. She said she understood. She felt the same way. That's why she had to stay.

The Vietnam war came along. Just before starting school, I dislocated my shoulder playing softball. Ran into a tree. Kept me out of the army and the war. I can't raise my arm above my head. Who wants a soldier who can't surrender?

Paul Godding got married young and had two kids so that kept him out.

Warren actually dropped out of college to enlist. Said that an artist has to experience life. Along with half of the neighborhood, I was at the airport to say good-bye to him. He told his parents not to worry, he'd only be gone a year. He was back in less than six weeks.

A few years ago, I was in Washington, D.C. Went to the War Memorial and ran my finger over his name. But you know, after Danny not much fazes me.

Paul Godding was in the minor leagues from the time he was eighteen until he was twenty-nine. Had a pretty good season his last year. But in the minor leagues, twenty-nine is an old, old man.

I saw him about a year after he got out of baseball when he came out to L.A. for a job interview. He gave me a call and we met for drinks.

Sitting across from Paul, listening to him talk. I am astonished by how little he has changed. Except for a few light lines around the eyes and another five pounds of muscle, he looks exactly the same as he did when I said good-bye to him in his bedroom eleven years ago.

Paul is talking but he is doing a monologue, not having a conversation. He neither expects nor is allowing for any comments on my part. He has already asked me what I've been doing for the past eleven years and has given me two words a year to tell it.

I am sitting at a small table in a bar on Wilshire Boulevard but Paul Godding is standing at the plate, at a Little League park that was torn down years ago, waiting for a seventeen-year-old pitch, which he will hit again, for the first grand slam home run of his career.

A few minutes later, standing at the plate in the last game of his high school career, he has just hit his third home run of the game.

Paul Godding is his own home movies. For a while, I am both fascinated and depressed by the fact that although it's been eleven years since I've last spoken to Paul, it's only been a few hours for him. He even bothers to mention, only half kidding, that I've never paid him back the sixty cents I borrowed the day before he left for the minors.

Gradually, though, the drinks dilute his dreams and his spirit sadly drifts down to the small table in the bar on Wilshire Boulevard.

"You know, Donny," Paul says as he runs his finger around the rim of his glass, "that insurance company that interviewed me today didn't care that I batted .294 last year." He chuckles softly at his own joke.

"I feel like I've lost eleven years of my life. I'm working two jobs just to make ends meet. Going to school part time, too. At the rate I'm going, I'll graduate from college the same year my kids do."

As the waitress walks by, Paul starts ordering another round but I stop him. "Paul, I'd love to stay and talk but I've got a meeting later this evening." Not true.

"Sure," says Paul. "I understand." I strongly suspect he does.

I look at the check and put down more than enough money to cover both the total and the tip. Paul doesn't object. Sixty cents earns a lot of interest in eleven years.

"Which way are you walking?" I ask him.

"I think I'm going to stay awhile."

"Oh . . . sure."

Standing up, shaking hands, saying our good-byes.

"We have to do this again, real soon," I say.

"Absolutely."

We both know we'll probably never see each other again. Walking away from the table, I hear Paul Godding ordering two more drinks, one for his friend.

Walking out the door and into the glossy Los Angeles night. Just needing to walk. Turning a corner and walking down a residential street.

Angry, really angry, at myself. Wondering how I could have wasted so many years of my youth dreaming of being a major-league baseball player. Wanting to make my living at a child's game. Such silliness.

Walking by a park. In the distant darkness, seeing the shadows of a diamond. Catching my imagination drifting back, punching the pocket of my glove, reaching up for that long, high fly ball . . . in front of thousands of fans . . . catching the last out of the big game.

Looking over my shoulder and seeing the late afternoon sunshine pale on the face of my house. Thinking of Brian. There are worse things than being an actor. There are worse things than being a dreamer.

When I glance at my watch, I remember, and the weight of the waiting falls on me again. Somehow, my mind has managed to forget, at least for a little while, that I have a long-distance call to make.

Picking up the spiral notebook and sticking the brown box under my arm. Standing and stepping up to the top of the porch. Sliding the key into the lock. Walking through the living room and back into the kitchen.

Gently setting the brown box down on the kitchen table as I take out the doctor's business card. Remembering what Danny had once said about dying. "It can't be that tough, I've never heard of anyone who couldn't do it." Feeling my stomach jump into my throat as I dial the number.

On the seventh ring, the phone is answered. It's Minnie.

"Hi, this is Donald Cooper . . ."

"Yes, Mr. Cooper, what can I do for you?"

Even though I realize that this may be, literally, a life-and-death phone call, the one-liner still jumps into my head. Thinking, Well, Minnie, I got a notice to renew my *Readers Digest* subscription and I was just wondering if I'm going to have time for all those points to ponder.

"Ah . . . you told me to call this afternoon to get the results of my test."

"Oh, of course, Mr. Cooper. Just a moment."

A hundred years later, she returns to the phone. "Your biopsy revealed that you have chondromas, which are benign tumors. Regardless, you should have them surgically removed at your earliest convenience."

"Is there any danger of them spreading?"

"Not that kind of tumor, Mr. Cooper. Have a nice day." Minnie doesn't wait for me to respond before she hangs up the phone.

Leaning against the counter, waiting for my body to float down from the high tide of adrenaline that has just now capped its surge through my body.

Getting ready to go. Picking up the brown box and then setting it down again. Slowly removing the cover. Looking. Touching. Remembering. Closing.

Taking the phone off the hook as I search my pockets for that small piece of paper with the number on it. Dialing. Hearing Ma say, "Hello."

"It's me, Ma."

"Oh, Donald, I'm so sorry I got angry with you."

"I'm sorry, too. Coming here kind of upset me."

"I understand, Donald."

"I know, Ma. You always understand. I'll be over in a few minutes."

"Oh, wonderful, honey."

"I checked the box. The wallet's there."

"You didn't have to do that."

"I know I didn't have to. I just knew you'd feel better if I did."

"Thank you, Donald."

"That's okay. I'll see you in a little while. . . ."

"Love you."

"I love you, too, Ma."

Picking up the brown box and taking one last look around at the kitchen. Hearing each voice just once more.

Walking through the living room. Dad's easy chair. The end of the couch where Ma always reads. The worn carpet where Danny used to sprawl in front of the television.

Stepping out on the porch and pulling closed the heavy door. Testing the handle to make sure it's locked. As I turn away, I hear the storm door clang shut behind me. Standing on the porch, looking out at the neighborhood.

Autumn. My favorite time of the year. But already it's getting dark. On Sunday afternoons, there'd be pyramids of burning leaves on the curb in front of every house. The men would be leaning on their rakes talking to one another and the kids would just be hanging around, savoring the fragrance of that autumn perfume as it drifted through the neighborhood. On Monday morning, on your way to school, you could still smell it in your jacket.

Then, a few years later, some jerk decided that burning leaves was bad for the environment and they passed a law against it. The guy probably lived in a high rise.

16

Late at night. Sitting at a small table in a motel room in Akron. The drapes are opened. All the light I need pours in from the parking lot.

Rita is sleeping. She has the blankets pulled up and tucked in around her. She is smiling. I have never thought about it before, but when Rita doesn't specifically choose another emotion, a smile is the one she naturally wears.

Opening the spiral notebook. Writing at the top of the page, "Chapter One." Skipping to the first line.

"There is a first time, and a last time, for everything. For snowfalls and funny faces. Kissing mirrors.

"And going home."